SHAKER

BLACKWINGS MC BOOK FIVE

BY

TEAGAN BROOKS

Cathy
♡ -Teagan Brooks

Dedication

To my husband,
for always listening to my scenes,
even when I know you didn't want to.

Contents

CHAPTER ONE

Keegan

Groaning, I rolled over and opened my eyes, despite the pounding in my skull. It took all of two seconds to realize I was not in my own bed. Quickly assessing the situation, I noted two important observations—I was dressed, and I was alone. But I had no clue where in the hell I was.

The room was nondescript with a full-size bed and minimal furniture. I didn't see any pictures or personal decorations to clue me in as to who owned the room. Slipping out of bed, I found my shoes and purse on the floor beside the door. I grabbed my purse and donned my shoes before yanking the door open and getting out of there.

Once in the hallway, I realized I was at the Blackwings MC Clubhouse. Flashes of the night before came to me as I made my way to the common room.

Harper inviting me to the club.

Tequila shots with Reese and Harper.

Duke, Carbon, and Shaker joining us.

More tequila shots.

Dancing.

Nothing.

From what I could remember, it seemed like I had a good time. I hoped I hadn't said or done anything embarrassing, especially since Duke was there. We already had enough issues at work.

The clubhouse was quiet. I had only been there a few times, and each time it was loud, even if only a handful of people were milling about. I didn't see a single person in the common room and took that for the blessing it was. Wasting no time, I headed straight for my car and peeled out of the gravel forecourt without looking back.

I did, however, glance at the clock in my car. Noting the time, I let loose a string of curses. I was already over an hour late, and I smelled like booze, sweat, and stale cigarette smoke. There was no way he would let this slide. I had to think of an acceptable excuse; one that wouldn't set him off.

I ran inside my apartment and straight to the shower to wash the previous night's stench from my body. Whisking my hair into a messy bun on top of my head, I threw on an outfit he would approve of, grabbed my stuff, and was back in my car within 10 minutes.

I drove a little over a half an hour until I reached what I hoped would be my saving grace. I pulled over on the side of the road and checked my phone. Just as I had hoped, I had no service. I had traveled this route many times and discovered early on that cell phone service was spotty at best for a good 10-mile stretch.

Sighing, I exited my car and rounded the hood. I pulled my knife from my purse and grimaced as I punctured the front right tire. The tires for my car weren't too expensive, but it was still money that I didn't want to spend; though, if this scheme worked, it would be worth it.

I situated my purse across my body and replaced my four-inch pumps with running shoes. Locking my car and praying my plan worked, I took off down the road, jogging at a quick pace. I had some time to make up for.

When he found out what happened, and he certainly would, I needed to be far enough down the road to account for the amount of time that had passed.

I was in decent shape and ran a few miles a day several times a week. I would do it every day if I could, but between my job and other obligations, I just didn't have the time. However, I was usually hydrated and well-rested when I went for a run. Currently, I was dehydrated, hungry, and massively hung-over.

My stomach started protesting first, churning and gurgling. I fought it as long as I could, but sooner than I'd hoped, I succumbed to the nausea and vomited what little was in my stomach on the side of the road. My stomach was empty, but my body didn't get the memo and continued with wretched dry heaving. It was at that point I realized I didn't have anything to drink with me. Digging through my purse produced a few breath mints. I popped one in my mouth and got back to it.

I made it at least another mile before I started to feel unbalanced. I stopped again and damn near fell on my ass when the world moved in unnatural ways. Well, now I really was in a mess. I was on the verge of collapsing on the side

SAVIOR
TEAGAN BROOKS

of the road from dehydration and overexertion, and I had no way to call for help. On the bright side, I guess this would account for the time I was trying to make up.

I staggered farther into the sparse grass on the side of the road and dropped to my knees. I vaguely heard the sound of an engine approaching as I fell face first into the unforgiving ground, embracing the blackness.

CHAPTER TWO

Shaker

When Phoenix dismissed Church, I went straight for my bike. I needed to ride and clear my head. He made some excellent points, but I still thought he was too hard on the girls, particularly Harper. She had been through hell at the hands of the Vine family and had a right to seek vengeance. I had been through some of my own shit due to two of the Vines. To say I was happy they were dead would be a vast understatement.

I told Phoenix I went down to the basement with the girls after I caught them sneaking down there to supervise and make sure no one got hurt. Truth be told, I was already on my way to the basement because I needed to rid the earth of the last living member of that vile family as much as Harper did.

Now that they were dead, I was left with feelings I didn't know how to process. Anger was the frontrunner. I was a fucking biker. How did some tiny little slip of a woman get the drop on me? A woman of no more than five feet three inches and 115 pounds managed to kidnap me and hold me hostage for five days. Needless to say, embarrassment was another emotion I was struggling to overcome. None of my brothers had given me any shit about it. Truthfully, they had been nothing but supportive, but I felt like they didn't see me the same as before.

I already had plenty of issues, more than my fair share, so being kidnapped by Hilarie/Valarie felt like Karma was dry fucking me for funsies. Actually, the kidnapping part wasn't what bothered me the most. The thing that bothered me the most was something that no one else knew about. Well, no one that was currently alive. I couldn't even bring myself to call it what it was in my mind, let alone say it to another person. The fact that her actions led to her discovery of my tightly kept secret infuriated me as much as it shamed me.

In what I first thought was a coincidence, but later turned out to be part of a well-executed plan, I met Hilarie at a bar in Cedar Valley. She wasn't the type of girl I usually fucked, but she approached me, and she seemed ready and willing, which meant I didn't have to work for it. We finished our drinks, left the bar, and I took her to the shithole apartment I kept in Cedar Valley. It was nothing more than a fuck pad; she knew it, and I didn't deny it. Everything had been going great; she was on her knees just inside the door swallowing my cock like it was going to shoot water from the fountain of youth down her throat. Then she stood and tried to kiss me. I. Do. Not. Kiss. She didn't like that very much, but accepted it for what it was. That should have been a red flag. When she accepted my next quirk without balking, it was a red flag that my dick-drained brain completely missed. As I said, I have issues, but with good reason.

***

Eight Years Ago
"Jacob, wake up," Beth gritted out while she shoved at my chest.
I yawned and rubbed the sleep from my eyes

as I sat up. "What is it?"

"We need to go to the hospital. My water just broke," she cried.

Her words had me instantly awake and alert. "Okay, I'm going to get dressed and put your bag in the car. Then, I'll come back and help you," I said as I rushed to pull on some clothes.

Beth was oddly quiet on the way to the hospital. Aside from the occasional moan from a contraction, she didn't utter a word. I figured she was as nervous as I was.

I don't remember the details after we arrived at the hospital. Everything happened so fast. Beth was taken to a room, and there was a constant flow of nurses and doctors coming and going. Before I knew it, they were saying it was time for her to push.

I dutifully stood by her side and held her hand while speaking words of encouragement into her ear. I wiped the sweat from her brow, fed her ice chips, kissed her cheeks, wiped her tears—you name it, I did it—because I loved her, and she was bringing our child into the world.

"You're doing great, Beth. The head is out. I just need one more big push from you," the doctor said.

Beth's face scrunched, and she squeezed the

hell out of my hand as she gave one final push.

Moments later, we heard a loud, angry cry and the doctor held up a screaming baby boy. A baby boy that was clearly not mine. There was no denying the prominent Asian features that did not come from myself or Beth, but I had a good idea who they did come from.

I turned my furious eyes to Beth. "How long have you been fucking your stepbrother?"

She gasped and tried to act like she was shocked by my question. "Jacob, I don't know—"

"Save it, Beth. You know exactly what I'm talking about."

Before I could continue, the doctor interjected, "If you would like to cut the cord, you need to do it now."

I held my hands up and waved him off, my disgust evident. "No, I'm not the father. I'm on my way out, so I'll send him in," I spat as I pushed through the door.

I walked out of her room, and I didn't stop my forward momentum until I reached the waiting room where our family and friends were gathered. The moment my eyes landed on Duc Phuc, her stepbrother, I was on the move again. "Congratulations, it's a boy," I spat and plowed my fist into his face. I heard him hit the floor, *followed by a few shocked gasps, as I walked out of the hospital, never looking back.*

I drove to the house I had been sharing with Beth since she told me she was pregnant with a singular focus. After turning off my phone, I got to work packing my personal belongings. Within an hour, I had everything loaded into my car and was on the highway headed south. Before I left the Marines, one of my buddies told me if I ever needed anything, he would do whatever he could to help me. I hoped he meant it, because I was about to take him up on that offer.

***

Carbon was happy to let me crash at his place while I figured my life out. Two weeks passed, and I still had no idea what I was going to do with myself when he told me about the club and invited me to a party at the clubhouse. From the moment I walked through the doors, I knew it was where I was meant to be.

Soon, I became a prospect for the club, and I busted my ass to get my patch. In less than a year, I received my patch and my road name, Shaker, for my ability to shake shit off. Two years later, I became the Road Captain for the Blackwings MC.

I pushed Beth's betrayal to the back of my mind and enjoyed the life of a single man.

Everything was going great, until it wasn't. I walked into the clubhouse one Friday afternoon to let Phoenix know I was going to spend the weekend with my mother. She must've been waiting for me because the second I stepped into the common room, she was in front of me.

"Shaker, I need to talk to you," Ashley demanded in her whiny voice.

"Later," I said dismissively and continued on the path to Phoenix's office. She was a club whore I fucked from time to time, but she had started to get a little clingy. Maybe it was time to cut her out of my rotation.

She grabbed my arm and pulled. "Shaker, I really need to talk to you."

I stopped but didn't turn to face her. "What?"

"Can we go somewhere and talk?"

Was she serious? "No, we fucking can't. We don't talk; we fuck. You're a club whore, Ashley, not an Old Lady. Don't forget that."

The desperation on her face quickly morphed into an angry scowl. "I'm well aware of my role here, Shaker. Sorry to bother you." She started to stomp away, but stopped after a few steps and threw over her shoulder, "I'm pregnant. It's yours."

Before I could process what she'd said and formulate a response, she was gone. I did what I did best; I shook it off. Then, I told Phoenix my plans and spent the next two days with my mother.

When I showed up at the clubhouse for the party the following Friday, Ashley was at the bar throwing shots back with the other club whores, and I saw red. Gripping her by her upper arm, I pulled her away out into the hallway.

"What the fuck do you think you're doing?" I demanded.

"Uh, what's it look like I'm doing?" she slurred.

"It looks like you're about to have your ass locked down. You can't be drinking and partying while you're pregnant."

Anger briefly washed over her face before she replaced it with a mask of indifference. "I guess it's good I'm not pregnant."

She tried to return to the bar, but I used my body to block her path. "Explain," I ordered. If she lied to me about being pregnant, she was going to get her ass kicked out and banned from the club. You couldn't mess with a brother like that without consequences.

"You didn't seem interested, so I had an

abortion. Problem solved," she said with a nonchalance that infuriated me.

"You heartless cunt!" I roared and punched the wall a little closer to her head than I'd intended. She let out an ear-piercing scream and dropped to the ground, curling in on herself.

"What in the fuck is going on out here?" Phoenix bellowed.

I sucked in a deep breath and tried to get my temper under control. Knowing Phoenix wouldn't wait long for a response, I held up one finger and began to pace. Finally, I managed to say, "She aborted a brother's kid without his agreement."

"Carbon, get her ass out of here," Phoenix said, clearly pissed.

I looked up to see Phoenix and Badger blocking the entrance to the hallway while Carbon physically removed Ashley from the premises. "I don't want to talk about it," I blurted.

Phoenix nodded. "We'll be at the bar if you change your mind."

A few days later, I found myself knocking on Byte's door.

He opened the door and gestured for me to come inside. "What's up, brother?"

"I was hoping you could help me find some information. It doesn't have anything to do with the club. It's personal, and I would like to keep it that way," I told him.

"Say no more. What am I looking for?" he asked with his hands poised at his keyboard.

I cleared my throat and looked around the room. I was extremely uncomfortable asking him to help me, but I needed to know. "I need to know if that club whore, Ashley, had an abortion last week."

If he was surprised by my request, he didn't let it show. He nodded and started typing. "I'll see if I can find some kind of proof for you, but I can already tell you she didn't have one. She was here every day last week doing what she usually does when she's here. She would've been away from the club for at least one or two days if she'd had an abortion."

"Fuck. So, she's still pregnant," I said, more to myself than to Byte.

"Or she never was," Byte added. "Get her ass in here and have Patch do a pregnancy test. If it comes back negative, take her to the cells and make her tell you the truth."

I clapped him on the shoulder and stood. "Thanks, brother. That's exactly what I'm going to do."

Being the dumbass that she was, Ashley

gladly came to the clubhouse when I called, and she was happy to submit to a pregnancy test, smirking at me the entire time Patch was drawing her blood.

She tried to talk to me while we were waiting for the results, but I was having none of it. At my request, Carbon escorted her to one of the empty rooms and locked the door from the outside.

Patch returned an hour later with the test results, and he gave it to me straight. "The test was negative. She's not pregnant now, and she wasn't pregnant last week either."

"You're sure?"

He nodded. "Yes, I'm sure. Even if she had an abortion last week, she would still have some of the pregnancy hormone known as hCG in her system. Her blood sample came back with an hCG level of zero."

"Thanks, Patch," I said and left the room with only one destination in mind.

Ashley flinched when I burst through the door. "I'm going to save us both some time and get right to it. I know you didn't have an abortion last week because I know you were never pregnant. The blood test Patch ran confirmed it. Why did you lie?"

Her mouth dropped open in surprise for a few

seconds before she brought her lips together and started spewing bullshit. Just like I thought she would. "I don't have to tell you shit."

"I'll pay you."

The scowl vanished from her face. "What?"

"You heard me. I'll pay you to tell me why you lied to me," I said calmly.

She blew out a long breath and said, "I found out who you are, and I thought I could get some money from you or get you to make me your Old Lady."

Motherfucking gold-digging bitches. "I see. So, here's what's going to happen. You're going to get the fuck out of here and never come back to this or any other Blackwings clubhouse. You're going to keep your mouth shut about what you think you know about me. If you don't, I'll kill you."

***

After what Ashley and Beth did, I made a promise to myself. I would never again allow myself to be put in that situation again. There was only one way to be absolutely certain I had not impregnated a woman no matter what she claimed. I solemnly swore I would not stick my dick in another pussy.

Honestly, I thought I had dealt with it and moved on. I didn't think about Beth or Ashley or feel any kind of heartache for either of them. The betrayal still stung, but it had faded over time. I kept my promise to myself and had not fucked a pussy in almost five years. I was by no means celibate, but I had rules, and the bitch could either abide by them or get the fuck out. Sexual relations with me consisted of my dick in a mouth or an ass, that's it. I didn't put my mouth anywhere on a woman's body, and I never touched anything other than her tits. She didn't touch me either as I required her hands to be bound behind her back. I wasn't taking any chances of a bitch smearing any of my seed in or around her tunnel of deceit. Like I said, issues.

At first, it was tough to keep my promise. I was a young, healthy, heterosexual male. In other words, I was horny, and I liked pussy, and there was plenty of it available at the clubhouse. As time passed, I morphed into an ass man. When I got myself off, the images in my mind had nothing to do with pussies. Eventually, the sight of one being fingered or fucked didn't even generate a twitch from my cock, which didn't bother me, until my encounter with a petite psycho.

When Hilarie kidnapped me and handcuffed me to the bed, she had one goal in mind. She had been begging me to fuck her cunt, and I had repeatedly refused, which pissed her off. I wouldn't give her what she wanted, so she decided she would take it. There she was, straddling my naked body with hers, desperately trying to get me hard. She tried everything, even using her mouth and rubbing her wet snatch all over my cock, but it didn't work. I knew what her end goal was, and my mind refused to let my body respond to her ministrations. I had known for a while that I didn't get hard for pussy, but this was a new revelation to her, and she was furious. Even though the bitch molested and abused my body against my will, I left that house with my dick still not having been in a pussy.

Movement on the side of the road caught my attention. I was so lost in my head I almost missed it. Almost. I pulled over and jumped off my bike. A few quick strides brought me to the woman I had just watched face plant on the side of the road. I gently nudged her with the toe of my boot. No response. I didn't want to touch her in case she was covered in something disgusting or had something on her that could connect me to the scene of a crime. Again, I didn't trust bitches.

Huffing in frustration, I nudged her again, "Hey! Girl! Can you hear me?" Nothing.

Grimacing, I dropped to a squat and carefully rolled her over. Pushing the hair from her face, I fell on my ass when I looked down at the beautiful face of Keegan Kensington. What in the hell was she doing out here? More importantly, what happened to her?

Gripping her shoulders, I shook her, "Keegan! Wake up!" A low moan was the only response I got from her. I didn't know what to do. Should I call an ambulance for her? Maybe call Phoenix first? Deciding to try to rouse her again before calling Phoenix, I shook her with a little more force. "Keegan!" I bellowed.

Her eyes shot open, filled with panic and fear. Recognition seemed to dawn on her face before she rolled to her side and vomited a small amount of bile and stomach acid, which landed on my thighs. Yuck.

I pulled out my phone and dialed Phoenix. "Prez, I found Keegan passed out face down on the side of Rocky Ridge Road. She's sort of awake now, but she's puking."

"Keegan? I thought she was still here. Hang on, brother," he said. "Huh, guess she left. Her car's gone."

"It's not here," I said.

"What?"

"Her car. It's not here. I don't recall seeing it along the road before I found her."

"Fuck!" he cursed. "Stay with her. I'm sending a cage."

I put my phone away and got to my feet. Walking to my bike, I rummaged in my saddlebags before returning to Keegan with a couple of bottles of water and some wet wipes. I uncapped the bottle and cupped her head, lifting it slightly. "Here, Keegan," I murmured and pressed the bottle to her lips, "try to drink some water."

She gingerly swallowed a few sips before pulling her mouth from the bottle. I continued to cup her head and used a wet wipe to clean the dirt from her face. She closed her eyes, and her body seemed to relax. At first, I thought that was a good sign but soon realized she hadn't relaxed, she had lost consciousness again. Feeling like an asshole, but at a loss for alternatives, I flattened my hand and slapped her across the face, not hard, but enough to sting.

The little hellcat's eyes opened, and she plowed her closed fist into the side of my face. It was weak given her current state, but I was still impressed with her response. "Easy, tiger. You were out again. I need you to stay awake until our ride gets here. How about some more water?"

She nodded and closed her eyes, but immediately opened them. "Sorry," I said sheepishly, "I didn't know what else to do." I took her small nod as acceptance of my apology. By the time Duke and Carbon arrived with the cage, she had managed to drink half the bottle of water but hadn't said a word. She had, however, grabbed onto my shirt and curled into my body.

To my surprise, Patch climbed out of the cage as well. He took one look at her and barked, "Get her in the cage, brothers, now." I scooped her into my arms and carried her to the SUV. Patch had folded the back seats down creating a large, flat area for him to work. I gently placed her in the center and slid my arms from underneath her.

Before I could move away, her hand shot out and grasped my wrist. With her eyes closed and her head turned in the opposite direction, she weakly uttered one word, "Stay."

Patch impatiently arched a brow as if to say, "Stay or go, but hurry the fuck up about it."

I sighed and tossed my keys to Carbon

silently asking him to ride my bike back to the clubhouse. With his nod, I climbed into the back beside Keegan. It wasn't until we pulled up at the clubhouse that I realized she had never let go of my wrist.

I carried her inside while Patch held the bag of fluid high in the air. He started an IV immediately and hooked her up to a bag of something he declared a necessity. I placed her on the stretcher in Patch's makeshift infirmary and looked up to see Phoenix's worried face.

"What're you thinking, Patch?" Phoenix asked.

"She's dehydrated, severely," he replied. "She'll need another bag of fluids, but should be fine after that. Her vital signs are already improving as well as her color. Was that her car with the flat tire?"

"Yeah," Phoenix answered. "I sent some boys to go get it."

Patch nodded, "Where Shaker found her was about six miles from the car."

"Seriously? Why the hell would she walk six miles instead of calling someone to come help her?" I asked.

"Because my phone doesn't get any reception on that part of Rocky Ridge Road," she answered then quirked her head. "How did you manage to get reception up there?"

I chuckled, "Byte worked some of his techy magic on our phones and boosted the antenna or something."

"Well, aren't you special," she snarked.

"Looks like you're getting some of your spunk back," Patch said.

Her cheeks flushed, "I'm sorry about all this. I didn't mean to be so much trouble."

"Nothing to be sorry for, darlin'. You needed some help, and we're helping you," Phoenix said. "Can you tell us what happened?"

"You know what they say, if it has tires or testicles, it's going to give you problems," she offered, causing us all to laugh.

When the laughter died down, Phoenix continued, "You aren't wrong. So, which one gave you trouble?"

She shifted on the stretcher and looked at her clasped hands resting in her lap. "Uh, I pulled over because I had a flat tire. When I realized I didn't have any cell phone reception, I figured the only thing I could do was walk until I found some to call for help. I didn't eat breakfast or anything before I left and with drinking so much last night, I guess it was too much for me."

Phoenix narrowed his eyes and studied her face. If I hadn't been watching them so closely, I would have missed it, the subtle shake of Keegan's head and the even more subtle nod in return from Phoenix. But I did see it, and to me, it meant one thing and one thing only; this bitch was hiding something, and I wanted no part of it. Just like that, I was out the door.

CHAPTER THREE

Keegan

Shaker bolted from the room like his ass was on fire. It shouldn't have offended me, but for some reason it did. It was nice of him to stop and help me, but he had no obligation to stay while Patch tended to me.

"Patch, can you give us a few minutes?" Phoenix asked.

Patch nodded and checked the IV and bag of fluids before silently leaving the room.

Phoenix stepped closer and pinned me with his piercing blue eyes. "You want to tell me what really happened?"

I sighed, "I was supposed to meet my family at an event this morning. I woke up late and rushed home to shower and change. Then, I got in my car and hauled ass. I must have hit something to cause the flat tire. When I realized I didn't have any reception, I started walking."

Phoenix didn't even try to mask his irritation with me. "I know roughly what time you left the clubhouse. There is no way you went home, showered, changed, drove to where we found your car, and walked six miles. Judging by the time and the state you were in when Shaker found you, I'd say you were running."

Well, shit. What could I say to that? I had barely been able to come up with the bullshit that landed me right back at the clubhouse. Swallowing thickly, I decided to give him a version of the truth. "I was running. Since I missed the event and didn't call, I knew my stepfather would be looking for me, and I was trying to get to where I could call him. Speaking of, do you know where my purse is?"

"Probably still in the cage. I'll go check."

My stepfather was going to be livid. Lawrence Prescott Hastings was not known for his patience or understanding. He gave orders and expected them to be followed. If they weren't, there would be consequences. We were to be seen as a picture-perfect family, regardless of what went on behind closed doors.

I knew what he would say when I called, no matter what explanation I gave him. He would prattle on and on about having to come up with an excuse for my absence that wouldn't tarnish our pristine image. There would be a few words about how I embarrassed him in front of whichever important group of people before he moved on to the insults and threats.

I hated him with a passion, and I hated myself for having to put up with him. If it weren't for my little sister, I would have told him to kiss my ass on his way to hell years ago.

Phoenix entered the room carrying my purse. He placed it on the stretcher beside me. "You need anything?"

"No, I'm okay. Thank you, for everything."

"You're welcome. Try to get some rest. Patch will be in to check on you soon," he said and left the room.

I dug through my purse and found my phone. The screen showed 17 missed calls. Shit. Taking in a deep breath, I braced for his wrath and tapped the screen.

"Keegan, how nice of you to call," Lawrence said in a tone that did not match his words.

"I thought you would want to know your

stepdaughter was found unconscious on the side of the road this morning and is currently hooked up to an IV," I spat.

"That sounds unfortunate. Am I to assume this is the reason for your absence this morning?"

"Yes, it is the reason for my absence. I got a flat tire on Rocky Ridge Road, and I didn't have any reception to call you or anyone else for help. I walked about six miles before I collapsed. Luckily, a friend happened to drive by and saw me," I told the heartless bastard.

"That sounds...convenient. One could assume you concocted that story in a weak attempt to excuse you from your obligation to this family," Lawrence drawled.

I used my phone to take a picture of me sprawled on the stretcher attached to an IV line and sent it to him. "Your proof is on its way," I said, forcing my tone to remain calm.

"It appears there is some truth to your story. It's just as well you weren't there if that's what you were planning to wear. Honestly, Keegan, I'm getting tired of you testing me. You know good and well what is expected of you, yet you constantly find ways to shirk your responsibilities. I do not like being forced to make up excuses on the spot for you. It is imperative that we maintain our family's image. When I married your mother, I had to accept you as part of the package, but your mother isn't here anymore, and I am finished with idly tolerating you. I expect to see you at the house by 6:00 pm this evening and please, dress appropriately."

He didn't give me a chance to reply before he disconnected. How did he expect me to get my tire replaced and drive to my family's home before 6:00 pm? I was still getting IV fluids. It didn't matter to him. I would have to figure it out. I had to meet his demands for the sake of my little sister. He had been using her to get me to bow to his wishes for years, and I had yet to find a way to get around him. Unfortunately, he was becoming more difficult to deal with every day that passed.

When Patch came in to check on me, he gave me some great news. The brothers had taken my car to the garage and replaced my tire for me.

"Do you know how much longer I will need to be here?" I asked, trying not to sound ungrateful.

"I want to get some more fluids in you. Maybe another hour," he said while replacing the depleted bag with a new one. "You should take it easy for the rest of the day and tomorrow, too."

"I will. I don't have any major plans," I lied.

True to his word, an hour later, Patch removed the IV and said I could go home. Unfortunately, he didn't think I should drive and arranged to have one of the members drive me home.

"I'll need my car for tomorrow," I hedged.

"Edge is going to follow and bring Coal back," he said. Oh, good. As soon as they left, I could grab my things and get on the road, which is precisely what I did 45 minutes later.

The drive to my stepfather's home was blessedly uneventful. When the house situated amid rolling green pastures came into view, I cringed. To anyone else, the sight would have been breathtaking. On the outside, I suppose it was. It was what was inside that house that I hated.

Lawrence's butler, Reginald, greeted me at the front door and led to my room with instructions to remain there until Lawrence called me for dinner. He also suggested that I use the time to freshen up my appearance. I didn't have the energy to respond to Reginald's snide remarks. All he got from me was a closed door in his face.

As much as I didn't want to, I showered and dressed in a different outfit for dinner. I pulled my hair back into a sleek chignon and kept my makeup light. I felt it was in my best interest to not anger the beast more than I already had.

Upon entering the dining room, my stepfather looked me over and said, "I see you are capable of choosing proper attire. Have a seat, Keegan. We have several things to discuss."

I sat and remained quiet. I had nothing to say to him that should actually be said. Folding my hands in my lap, I kept my eyes cast down and waited for him to start.

"As I said earlier, I'm tired of your behavior. I have more important things to do with my time than to deal with you. After giving it some thought, I've decided it is time for you to become someone else's problem. I have arranged for you to be married in three months. Your courtship with Preston Hensley will begin this evening," he proudly informed me.

What. The. Fuck.

"Excuse me," was all I could manage after the bombshell he dropped.

"You will marry Preston Hensley after a short yet public courtship. He and his family are joining us for dinner this evening."

"You can't do this," I gritted out, fighting back the tears.

"Stupid girl. It's already done," he said.

"Where is Gabriella?" I asked.

"She should be getting settled into her room at Wexington Academy right about now. Had you attended our scheduled luncheon, you would have been able to say goodbye. She was quite crushed when her sister didn't bother to come to her going away soirée," he said with a devious smile.

He sent her away to boarding school. She was only five years old. She was probably scared and had no one to comfort her. And he let her think I didn't care about her. Fuck this shit. I rose to my feet and squared my shoulders, "Fuck you, and fuck your planned marriage."

I pushed back from the table and moved toward the stairs. I was getting my things and getting the hell out of that house. I was almost to the stairs when a hand fisted in my hair and yanked me backward. I stumbled a few steps before I could regain my footing.

A fist crashed into my cheek, knocking my head to the side only to be met with another fist. He delivered two more blows to the side of my head before I dropped to the ground and tried to shield my face with my hands.

With my arms covering my head, my torso was wide open for his assault. The first kick to my stomach knocked the air from my lungs. The second kick had me rolling to the side as I gasped for air. But when he slammed his heel into my back, directly over my kidney, I wondered if he was going to kill me. I lost track of the blows after that.

Finally, he decided I'd had enough and ordered me to get up to my room and stay out of sight. He didn't want his dinner guests to catch sight of me.

Somehow, I managed to make it to my room. I could feel my face swelling, and I was certain a rib or five were cracked. I took a few minutes to wallow in the pain before I pulled myself together enough to get the hell out of there.

I knew Reginald would be busy serving dinner, and I knew where the attendant kept the keys to the vehicles. Carefully, I crept down the back staircase and slipped through the kitchen to get to the back door. From there, I scurried the short distance to the detached garage. As expected, the keys were hanging on a hook right inside the door. I grabbed the set for my car and went back outside where my car was parked. Thankfully, it wasn't blocked in by any other vehicles.

Something to my left caught my attention. I

turned to look and saw Reginald barreling toward me. I yelped and painfully dashed for my car. I jerked the door open and all but fell into the seat. Scrambling to close the door and hit the locks, I managed to narrowly evade Reginald. I couldn't stop myself from sticking out my tongue as I sped away from the pompous red-faced butler.

Once I was a safe distance from the house, I pulled over on the side of the road. I just needed a minute to get a handle on the pain before I could continue. A quick rifle through my purse produced some ibuprofen. After swallowing those, I forced myself to start driving again. I knew the pain was likely going to get worse, and I didn't want to be stuck anywhere other than my own home.

After a grueling drive back to my house, I drug myself inside and managed to make it to the bed before I collapsed.

CHAPTER FOUR

Shaker

Fucking Keegan. Her wallet had fallen out of her purse when we were transporting her back to the clubhouse. Somehow, I was volunteered to return it to her because, apparently, I passed her place on the way to my own.

I pulled into her driveway and grimaced before climbing off my bike. With any luck, I could hand her the wallet and leave with little to no chit-chat. I knocked on her door and waited. Nothing. I knocked one more time before resorting to pounding on the door. Finally, I heard footsteps moving toward the door. Keegan pulled the door open with a barked, "What?"

"What the fuck happened to you?" I roared. Her beautiful face was swollen and bruised, complete with the remnants of dried blood under her nose. She flinched, and I watched in horror as she wrapped her arms around her waist and groaned. I stepped forward without a word, and she instinctively moved back.

Once inside, I closed her door and gently led her by her shoulders to her couch. She gingerly sat and placed a hand over her face. "Keegan, what in the hell happened to you?"

Tears poured from her eyes. "It's nothing. Really. I'm fine. Why are you here?"

"Bullshit! Someone beat the hell out of you, and I want to know who the fuck it was," I barked.

"Leave."

"Fuck, no. I can't leave you like this," I said.

"Please," she begged, "just go."

I didn't understand it, but I felt a deep primal need to comfort her, to protect her. If I was honest with myself, I felt it the day before, too, but I tried my best to ignore it. I carefully sat beside her and lowered my voice, "Keegan, baby, who did this to you?"

She only cried harder. "Have you seen a doctor?"

Her panicked eyes met mine, "No. No doctor."

"Are you going to let me look you over?" I asked.

She grimaced and then blew me away when she uttered, "Fine." She stood and untied the robe she was wearing, letting it fall to the floor, leaving her standing in front of me in nothing but a skimpy pair of panties.

Being the asshole that I was, my eyes immediately went to her full tits and her perfectly pink nipples. To my utter surprise, the sight had my dick twitching.

Then, my gaze dropped to the obvious shoe shaped bruise over her ribcage, and my fury blazed once again. That was probably the first kick and had caused her to roll because her other side was one big bruise that wrapped all the way around to her back.

I stood, towering over her, and tenderly cupped her battered cheeks in my hands, whispering, "Just give me a name, and I'll kill him."

She shook her head, "I can't."

"Can't? Or won't?"

"Both," she whispered.

I dropped my hands and took a step back to scoop her robe from the floor. Carefully placing it around her shoulders, I pleaded, "At least let me help you."

She chewed on her bottom lip before giving me a curt nod. "Go get into bed, and I'll bring you some painkillers and something to eat."

What in the hell was I doing? I was just doing what anyone else would do, right? No, I was getting involved in a situation that was none of my business. I pulled out my phone and placed a call, hoping I wasn't making a mistake.

By the time I had put together a sandwich and some chips for Keegan, I heard a soft knock on the door. I yanked it open to find Harper flanked by Carbon.

"What's going on, Shaker?" Harper asked.

Shit. I thought she would come alone. I nervously glanced at Carbon and back to Harper, "Uh, Keegan needs you. She's in her bedroom. Can you take this to her?"

She gave me a quizzical look, but took the plate and walked into Keegan's room. The sound of the plate crashing to the floor accompanied by Harper's cry had Carbon knocking me out of his way and rushing to his woman.

"Fuck!" he hissed.

"Out! Now!" Harper ordered, shoving him back with her little hands.

"Brother?" he asked.

I shook my head. "I don't know anything. I came to drop off her wallet and found her like that. She won't tell me what happened or who did it. She didn't want to go to the hospital, but she did let me look at her. Fuck, brother, she has a shoe print on her side. The other side is one massive bruise. I didn't know what to do, so I called Harper for help."

"Sounds like it was someone she knows. If it was a random attack, she would have said so or reported it. Do you think she was, uh, violated?" he asked.

A sharp pain shot through my chest. "I didn't ask that, but she wasn't shy about showing me her body. Who the fuck would have done that to her?"

"No idea, man. I've never heard her mention a boyfriend. You think this has anything to do with how we found her yesterday?"

"Yeah, I do. I don't know how, but I think it's connected."

Keegan's cell phone lit up and started buzzing on the coffee table. Carbon picked it up and arched a brow. He turned the screen toward me. "Jackass calling" flashed on the screen.

I snatched the phone and accepted the call, "Yeah."

"Put Keegan on," a man said with an arrogance that could only be mustered by an abundance of money.

"And whom shall I say is calling?"

"Keegan. Now," he ordered.

"One moment please," I said and pressed mute. Looking at Carbon, I said, "I think we have our answer. Save this number." I rattled off the number on the screen before heading to Keegan's room.

Harper opened the door when I knocked. Holding up the phone, I said, "She has a phone call." I assumed Harper would take the phone and give it to Keegan, but she moved to the side and gestured for me to enter.

When Keegan looked at the screen, her face tightened and a silent curse left her lips. She closed her eyes and slowly raised her phone to her ear, "Hello."

The sound of an angry male voice echoed around the room. When one tear rolled down her cheek, I snapped. I snatched the phone from her hand and put it to my ear, "...or you will regret ever crossing me, you worthless little cunt."

"Care to repeat that? I didn't catch the first part," I spat.

"I am not in the habit of repeating myself nor

do I care to speak to someone with whom I am not acquainted."

"My apologies. Allow me to introduce myself. I'm Shaker, Road Captain of the Blackwings MC, original chapter."

He cackled into the phone. "Keegan has taken up with a biker gang. I should have expected as much from the little whore. Enjoy her while you can, the clock is ticking."

I didn't realize I had been pacing while he was talking. I turned around to find Keegan quietly crying in Harper's arms. Harper stared at me with wide, fear-filled eyes.

I slowly approached the bed and took a seat at the foot. "Keegan, I'm going to find out who that was, but it would make things a lot easier if you would tell me."

CHAPTER FIVE

Keegan

Overwhelmed didn't even begin to describe how I was feeling. I wasn't even completely awake when I opened the door to Shaker. The next thing I knew, Harper was pushing Carbon out of my bedroom and coaxing me to tell her what happened. Before I could get started, Shaker was barging in with my phone, and now they all knew more than I ever wanted anyone to know.

"Shaker, I appreciate the concern, but I don't need you to be my knight in shining armor. I can handle this."

"Oh, sweetheart, I'm no knight, but I can't ignore this. Even if I could, Carbon wouldn't."

I sighed, exasperated with the whole situation, "If you must know, that was my stepfather, Lawrence Prescott Hastings, III. Perhaps you've heard of him?"

Shaker's brows furrowed, "Senator Hastings is your stepfather?"

"So, you have heard of him," I snarked.

Shaker stood and placed his balled fists on his hips, "He did this to you? Why?"

"Because I refuse to willingly be his puppet. The only reason I comply with any of his demands is so I can see my little sister. I can't let him hurt her. She's only five years old," I said, before choking on a sob.

"What did he mean when he said the clock was ticking?"

"Apparently, he has arranged a marriage for me that is set for three months from now. You can see for yourself how well he tolerated my refusal," I said, waving my hand from head to toe.

Shaker patted my lower leg, "I'll be back."

I turned to Harper, "Where is he going?"

She shrugged, "My best guess is to call Phoenix."

"Fuck!" I swore and grimaced from the pain caused by my muscles tensing. "I don't want the club involved in this."

"It doesn't look like you have a choice at this point," Harper replied.

"If I don't do what he asks, he won't let me see my sister. He's already shipped her off to a boarding school. She's too young for that!" I shrieked.

"Where's your mom?" Harper asked.

"She died while giving birth to my little sister. She never even got a chance to hold Gabriella. After a difficult delivery with me, the doctors advised her not to have any more children, but Lawrence insisted they have a child of their own, no doubt to boost his political career. She foolishly agreed and left an innocent little girl in the hands of a monster." I hated talking about my mother. She knew the risks and did it anyway. She honestly believed it wouldn't happen to her. Much to her surprise, she was one of those that made up the unfavorable portion of statistical data.

"It's okay to be angry with her. She left you, too," Harper said quietly. Her words sent me into another fit of tears, angry tears. I had never permitted myself to be upset with my mother for putting herself in a situation that resulted in her death. To have someone tell me it was okay was like lifting the floodgates for emotions I had been holding in for years.

Harper sat silently with her arms around me and let me cry until Shaker reentered the room. "Has he done this before?" I nodded. He had "taught me a lesson" several times before. I hoped Shaker didn't want me to tell him the details about each one of those instances.

"Have you ever tried to press charges?" he asked in a way that made me think he already knew the answer.

I scoffed, "Seriously? If you know how to press charges against a senator, please let me know." In all honesty, I hadn't ever actually tried to press charges because I knew it would be a futile attempt. He would grease some palms, and all would get swept under the rug.

"Fair enough," Shaker replied, catching me off guard. I was expecting him to argue with me and give me a speech about no one being above the law. That's the typical response from someone who isn't familiar with the inner workings of the dark side of the upper crust. Being a biker, he probably knew things most of the general population didn't.

"Here are your options—you can stay at the clubhouse, or you can stay here and have one of the brothers present around the clock," Shaker said.

My jaw dropped. "Neither. I don't want the club involved in this. My stepfather is not going to go out of his way to come after me. He never has. As long as I stay away from his house, he won't bother me. Gabriella is away at school, so that gives me some time before I have to interact with him again."

"If you don't want to make the decision, I'll make it for you," Shaker snapped.

"I'm staying here in my own home, and no one is staying with me," I gritted out.

"Keegan, I'm not agreeing or disagreeing with the protection order, but I don't think you should stay by yourself tonight because of your injuries. You could spend the night with me and Carbon. Or, I could stay here with you, but after all this, Carbon would insist upon staying, too. After you've had some rest, we could continue this discussion," Harper interjected.

My shoulders slumped, "I could use some help with a shower and getting changed. You really wouldn't mind staying here?"

"Of course not. Like I said, my big scary biker is going to insist on staying, but he'll stay out of your hair," Harper said with a grin.

I knew she was only delaying the inevitable, but I was grateful for it. Perhaps with some rest, I would be able to think of a way to talk the bikers into backing off. Then, I could focus on dealing with Lawrence.

Harper helped me shower and get changed into something much more comfortable. She did insist that we take photographs of my injuries in case we later needed proof. I tried to protest, but she was having none of it. Finally, I sucked it up and let her take the damn pictures. It wasn't like anyone was ever going to see them.

At some point between the photographs and the shower, Harper called Patch and sent Carbon out for supplies. Before helping me get dressed, she painfully, albeit carefully, wrapped a brace around my torso. Then, she fed me, tucked me into bed, and instructed me to sleep. She perused my movie collection and selected one to pop in, but I couldn't tell you which one it was because I was asleep before it ever started to play.

Something cold and wet was touching my arm. When I tried to brush it away, nothing was there. As soon as I put my hand down, there it was again. I gingerly rolled to my side and opened my eyes. Then, I let out a blood-curdling scream.

Crying out in pain, I did my best to plaster myself against the headboard of my bed, drawing my knees to my chest. My bedroom door nearly flew off the hinges when Carbon pushed through. I was too scared to say anything, so I just pointed at the giant black beast standing beside my bed.

Carbon chuckled, "There's no need to be scared of him. You've never met Titan before?"

I frantically shook my head. "What is it?"

He laughed loudly at that. "He's Harper's dog, a Cane Corso. He's a licensed protection dog." He turned his attention to the beast, "Titan, I think you scared Keegan. Were you nudging her to get some attention?"

I wouldn't have believed it if I hadn't seen it with my own eyes. I still wasn't sure I believed it. The beast bobbed its head up and down twice like he was answering yes to Carbon's question. "Did he just—?"

Carbon grinned, "Yeah, he's a smart boy. Sorry he scared you. Harper's cousin is here, and I guess Titan felt like he wasn't getting enough attention. It doesn't matter if you're awake or asleep, he'll nudge you with his nose until he gets what he wants."

"Why is Harper's cousin here?" I asked.

"He's installing a security system for your house," he said.

"What?" I shrieked.

"He's the best in this area. Not sure if you've met him before or not. He's with the Devil Springs chapter. His name's Judge, looks a lot like Duke."

"Why is he installing a security system in my house?" I asked, getting slightly irritated with the way these men had barged in and taken over.

"Because you didn't have one, and even though you're in a situation you can't handle on your own, you're going to fight letting the club help you. This way, at least we know your home is safe," he said. I wanted to be pissed at his words, but he was right on two counts—I was going to fight their help, and I couldn't handle Lawrence on my own. That didn't mean I wasn't going to try though.

CHAPTER SIX

Shaker

I had developed what I could only describe as an unhealthy obsession with Keegan. Not in the way that most people obsess over another person. I didn't have daydreams about our future together or covertly follow her around to see if she was seeing anyone. I didn't have any romantic feelings for her. Sure, she was hot as fuck, but there was no way I was exposing her to my issues with her as close to the club as she was. I didn't want my shit broadcast around the club.

No, I was obsessed with her situation. Obviously, her stepfather had a reason behind trying to force her hand in marriage, and I had never known of a situation like that where the reason was anything other than corrupt. I wasn't as good as Byte with computers, but I could do some decent digging. However, I couldn't manage to dig up shit on her stepfather. I knew it wasn't because he was squeaky clean. No, it was because it was well hidden. What I could find of his financials appeared to be in order. He wasn't up for reelection in the near future. He wasn't being accused of participating in any scandal of sorts. Still, I knew he was hiding something, and I was going to find it or die trying.

I still had one major card up my sleeve, though I was holding onto it as long as I could. Once I played that card, there would be no going back. While it would likely get me most or all of the answers to my questions regarding Senator Hastings and his activities, it would expose a part of my life that I had managed to keep hidden from my brothers. I had a feeling Phoenix, and maybe Badger, knew from having me checked out when I became a prospect. They never asked anything, and I didn't volunteer any information, because really, it wasn't relative to the club nor would it impact the club in any way.

I thought about asking Byte to help me do some digging, but I didn't want to explain why I was asking. Hell, I didn't even know the answer to that myself. I wasn't one of those people who couldn't let something go. I was okay not knowing the answer to a question. I could put a book down halfway through. I could walk away without placing the last piece of a puzzle. So, not only was her situation bugging me, but the fact that it was bugging me was bugging me.

It had been two weeks since I knocked on Keegan's door and found her beaten and bruised. I hadn't seen her or heard anything about her in those two weeks. I didn't even have the urge to ask about her, so why in the hell was I so obsessed with her problems?

A shoulder softly bumping mine brought me back to the present. Harper dropped into a chair beside me and propped her face in her hands, "What's wrong, friend?"

A small smile appeared on my face at her calling me friend. Harper and I had developed a unique, and somewhat unexpected, friendship after being kidnapped and escaping together. We also tortured and killed one of our kidnappers together. She was one of a handful of females that I didn't see as a hole. "Nothing. Just thinking. How've you been? Staying out of trouble?"

She rolled her eyes, "I don't have a choice.

I have to stay out of trouble." She paused and opened her mouth like she was going to say something and then seemed to decide against it. I frowned. She didn't need to censor her words around me. Her eyes darted around, and she lowered her voice, "Have you talked to Keegan?"

"No," I answered, confused. "Why would I talk to Keegan? We aren't friends."

She shrugged, "Oh, it seemed like you two were friends."

She moved to stand, but I stopped her. "What would you have said if I said yes?"

She sighed and slumped back into her chair. "She's attending a charity ball next weekend... because her stepfather said her presence was required. I know she said he wouldn't do anything to her in public, but I'm worried about her. I tried to talk her out of it, but she said she has to go."

"Harper, listen to me. You can only help people who want to be helped. She knows the risk she is taking, and she's still deciding to take it. The best thing you can do is be there for her when things go to shit. Because they will go to shit before it's over with."

"That's pretty much what Carbon said, too. Well, I better get back to cleaning if I want to get out of here before the debauchery begins," she said, heading back to the bar with her bucket of cleaning supplies. She and two other Old Ladies had broken a few serious rules and were being punished. Part of their punishment was keeping the clubhouse clean. I did feel bad for them, but at least Phoenix didn't kick them out of the club. He couldn't have even if he had truly wanted to because one of the Old Ladies was none other than his own wife and Old Lady.

I sat back and drained my beer, trying to decide what to do with the rest of my evening. I wasn't interested in staying for the debauchery Harper referred to either. It wasn't going to be anything special, just the usual crowd drinking and fucking the club whores and hang around skanks. It dawned on me that I hadn't picked up a bitch in a few weeks. Maybe that's what was wrong with me. I needed to get off. Well, that was an easy problem to fix. I stood and made my way to my bike.

Three hours later, I was sitting in a bar in Cedar Valley nursing a beer and wondering why I was thinking about a damn charity ball instead of picking up a piece of ass as planned. I had even brushed several bitches off. Something was seriously wrong with me. My next move further supported my self-assessment.

I pulled out my phone and dialed, "Hey, I need your help with something."

***

As expected, my request was quickly and easily filled with little fuss and minimal questions. I was glad for that because I wasn't sure I would be able to provide answers had there been questions. Even as the car was pulling up, I still hadn't decided if I was going to make myself known or wait and see if I was discovered. Either way, if I was spotted and identified by one particular guest, the card I was holding on to would be well and truly played.

Moments before the door opened, I slid the mask over my face and smoothed a hand over my hair. The driver opened the door, and I stepped out into the very different world of society's upper class. It had been years since I had attended any kind of social event, yet absolutely nothing had changed. The proud men parading trophy wives around the room, the bitter divorcees sneering while clutching martini glasses, the up and coming socialites trying to stand out above all the others, the young bachelors discussing business, and the old money watching as the first act of the live play they had created began.

Knowing I would need it to withstand the next few hours, I went straight to the bar and got a drink. Downing it immediately, I ordered a second and started to move around the room without being noticed, a skill well-honed after years of practice only made easier by the masquerade theme. My face was hidden behind an intricately woven full-face mask, which was just long enough to conceal the sliver of tattoos that peeked out from the collar of my dress shirt. It also had a thin layer of mesh to obscure my eyes. As long as I remembered to keep my voice in low, hushed tones, I felt certain no one would recognize me.

I quietly studied the room, hovering in the background, for over an excruciatingly long hour when I finally spotted Senator Hastings talking with a man and woman who appeared to be around his age and a younger woman, I assumed to be the couple's daughter. I scanned the area around them and didn't see anyone that resembled Keegan. Maybe she came to her senses and decided not to come.

I maneuvered my way through the various clusters of snotwads until I was standing within earshot of the good senator. They were discussing a recent deal they had reached when the woman subtly nudged the man presumed to be her husband with her elbow. He cleared his throat and abruptly changed the subject to the senator's horse farm.

I didn't have to wonder long why they changed topics so quickly. The senator and the couple parted to reveal what had to be the couple's son approaching. He strutted up to them like a proud peacock, and I was overcome with the urge to snap his neck.

"Where is Keegan?" the senator asked, failing to hide his displeasure.

"She excused herself to the ladies' room," the prick said.

I was moving before I knew what I was doing. No longer concerned about going unnoticed, I pushed straight through the crowd toward the restrooms. The noise significantly quieted when I exited the ballroom and died out completely when I rounded the corner, and there she was. Keegan.

She was leaning against the wall at the end of the corridor gazing into the night sky through the floor to ceiling windows. She was a hauntingly beautiful sight. Her black gown bared her shoulders and molded to her body perfectly down to her feet where it flared just enough to allow her to walk. Her raven colored hair was swept to the side and secured with a jewel-encrusted clasp to frame her beautiful face partially hidden by a lacy black mask accented with crystals that matched her pale blue eyes. The deep red staining her lips and the lone tear sliding down her cheek completed the picture of a beautiful broken angel.

She didn't notice me approaching until I was within arm's reach. She gasped when she finally saw me and turned to face me. Without a word, I cupped her cheek and wiped the tear away with my thumb. Letting my hand slide from her cheek, down her arm, I clasped her hand in mine. With a small tug, she followed as I led her into the ballroom and onto the dance floor.

I placed my hand on her waist and stared into her eyes, waiting for her permission. She nodded once, and then we were moving. Eyes locked on mine, her body followed me as if we had been dancing together for years. The song ended far before I was ready to let her go, so I didn't. I tightened my grip on her waist and waited. When the next song began, I cocked my head to the side. She graced me with a shy smile, and we were moving again.

Four dances later, she was smiling brightly, still holding my gaze. Her cheeks had a slight flush to them, and her eyes had brightened. With only our hands touching, the woman had me captivated. For the briefest of moments, I forgot where I was, forgot about my past, forgot about everything except her.

The sound of a throat clearing broke the spell. We paused mid-step, and I turned my head toward the sound. The young man I saw earlier with Senator Hastings gave me a pointed look. "May I cut in?" he asked, though it wasn't a question. I didn't want to let her go, especially not to him, but I wasn't going to draw attention to myself. I gave him a sharp nod before stepping toward Keegan. I placed a soft kiss on her cheek and whispered, "It was a pleasure." With that, I backed away, slowly disappearing into the crowd.

In need of another drink, I headed to the bar only to be stopped when a dainty hand reached out and grasped my forearm. I turned quickly and came face to face, well her face to my chest, with my mother. "Don't look so frightened, dear. I have no intentions of revealing your identity. I only wanted to say hello."

I covered her hand with mine and placed a kiss on her cheek, "Hey, Mom. You look beautiful this evening."

"Thank you. Who was the lovely lady I saw you dancing with?" she asked.

"I didn't get her name," I hedged.

"Jacob," she started with sadness in her eyes.

"Don't. Not here. Besides, I already know what you're going to say." She was going to tell me that I needed to let go of the past and find a nice girl to move on with. That not all girls were like the cunt that shall not be named. I never told her about the second one that screwed me over, and there was no way she would ever know about the kidnapping.

"Very well. My only wish is for you to be happy," she said with a forced smile. "Go on, before someone sees us talking."

"Thanks, Mom. Love you," I said and continued to the bar. I should have expected my mother to show up after I called and asked her to have me added to the guest list, particularly since she didn't demand to know why I wanted to attend.

I lingered at the bar for the remainder of the night. I didn't want to go back into the ballroom, but I wasn't ready to leave either. It had nothing to do with wanting to see Keegan again. I needed to get my shit together. What was I going to do, sit there until I saw her leave with her stepfather or another man? Disgusted with myself, I got up to use the restroom before calling for my car.

I stepped into the stall to piss, since my pierced cock would have me standing out like a sore thumb if someone glanced, and these insecure fuckers were known to glance.

"Why are you even bothering? You don't have to put in any effort, son. It's already a done deal," a man said.

"I figured she would be more cooperative if she liked me, as much as I would enjoy her fighting," the son chuckled sinisterly.

"Save that for later. For now, it needs to appear that the two of you are falling in love. Are you taking her home tonight?"

"No. Senator Hastings thought that would be too forward and could lead to gossip. He's escorting her home."

Oh, no, the fuck he was not. I burst out of the stall and shoved past them. I had to find her before she left with him. He would no doubt lay into her for dancing with me. I wouldn't allow him to hurt her because of me.

I rushed down the corridor and rounded the corner, coming to a sudden stop when I saw Keegan talking to none other than my mother. I didn't know if I should hug her or strangle her as I had no doubt she intentionally sought out Keegan. Senator Hastings was standing with them, also speaking to my mother. Did she know them? It hadn't crossed my mind, but it wasn't out of the realm of possibilities.

I slowly approached them, unsure of how I was going to get Keegan away from the senator and keep my identity from being revealed. My mother smiled brightly when she saw me approaching. "I know it is late, but it would please me to no end if you would join me for a nightcap. It has been such a long time since I've had the opportunity to enjoy such pleasant company. Senator Hastings, with your permission of course. I will ensure that she arrives home safely," she nodded toward the men strategically positioned behind the senator. "I have my own security team as well."

The senator grimaced, but had to relent. My mother had backed him into a corner using nothing more than good manners and kind words. "I see no reason to deny a lady's wishes. Please enjoy the rest of your evening. Keegan, I will see you in the morning for breakfast."

After giving Keegan a pointed look, the senator turned to leave, and I took the final steps to reach my mother and Keegan. My mother smiled again, "Please excuse me. I need to powder my nose before we take our leave. Jacob, will you escort Ms. Kensington to the car? I will be along momentarily."

Stunned by my mother's behavior, I nodded once and extended my bent arm for Keegan. She looped her arm through mine and allowed me to lead her to my mother's waiting limousine. Once inside, she sat facing me, "You're Jacob Marks?" I nodded. "As in the never seen, never heard from son of Jacquelyn Kingsley Marks and the late Jacob Harvey Marks?" I nodded again. How did she know my family?

She grinned and extended her hand, "It's a pleasure to meet the exclusive, elusive Jacob Kingsley Marks. I'm Keegan Quincy Kensington."

I took her hand in mine, turned it slightly, and placed a kiss to the top of her hand, letting my lips linger a few beats longer than necessary. I was going to have to speak, and as soon as I did, she would recognize my voice. I raised my covered eyes to meet hers and opened my mouth to say something when she placed one finger over my lips and shook her head. "Don't.

I'm rather enjoying the mystery you've created around yourself. That's not an easy feat, and I would like to savor it a bit longer."

Part of me wanted to laugh. I didn't intentionally set out to shroud myself in mystery. Quite the opposite, actually. I never really cared for the high society lifestyle, so, when I left, I never came back. Then, I grew into my baby face, got a few piercings, got a lot of tattoos, lost the military haircut, and put on a good 30 pounds of muscle, and people just didn't recognize me anymore.

Even with my eyes locked on hers, I was lost in my thoughts, so I hadn't noticed how she'd moved closer to me while speaking. Her mouth was less than an inch from mine. I could feel the soft puffs of air escaping from her parted red lips. She leaned even closer, watching me watch her. She ever so softly placed her lips against mine, in the barest of touches, and I flinched away from her.

"I'm so sorry," she whispered. "I shouldn't have..."

It was an automatic reaction on my part. I had been dodging kisses for over five years. No one had gotten anywhere near as close as she had. And I wanted more. In a flash, I gripped the nape of her neck and pulled her to me, fusing my lips with hers. When she didn't pull away, I pressed harder against her mouth and thrust my tongue inside.

Her mouth was warm and wet, and after years of going without, I jumped back in with both feet, putting everything I had into that kiss. My control almost slipped when she moaned into my mouth. I was seconds away from hoisting her into my lap when I heard a soft tap on the window. We jerked back from each other like two teenagers getting caught by their parents. The door opened, and my mother slid into the seat across from us. She looked from me to Keegan and back. Smiling she said, "Oh, good, my plan worked. Now, wipe that lipstick off your mouth, son; it's not your color."

CHAPTER SEVEN

Keegan

I blamed stress for my actions. Otherwise, I had no excuse for shamelessly kissing a man I knew nothing about other than his name. I hadn't seen his face and had only heard his voice in a whisper. There was something familiar about him though. I felt at ease around him, and oddly enough, I felt safe, which was damn near unachievable in Lawrence's vicinity.

The evening had been no less than horrible. After suffering through dinner with Preston Hensley and his parents, as well as Lawrence and his ridiculously young date, I then had to pretend to enjoy their company at the charity ball. Nearing my breaking point, I excused myself to the ladies' room for a few minutes of peace when the man in the intriguing mask approached me and wordlessly led me to the dance floor.

I wanted to scream when Preston cut in. Instead, I focused on the tingling sensation the mystery man's lips left behind when he lightly kissed my cheek. Or I tried to, but Preston's relentless questions accompanied by his lack of dance skills stole what little happiness I had managed to find for myself. By the fifth time he asked me who I was dancing with, even though I had already told him I didn't know, I waited for the song to end and left the dance floor.

Of course, returning to Lawrence and the Hensleys was no better. Lawrence refused to let me have more than two glasses of wine. Not only did I have to tolerate the dreadful company, but I also had to do it sober. I was contemplating faking a violent case of diarrhea when a regal looking middle-aged woman approached us. She introduced herself as Mrs. Jacquelyn Kingsley Marks. Recognition dawned upon hearing her name.

Mrs. Marks had been friends with my mother. I hadn't seen her in years, well before Mom died. I had finished high school early and was off to college immediately so I could get away from

Lawrence. Everyone seemed to have scattered from Mom's life when Lawrence entered the picture.

Much to my delight, Mrs. Marks all but ignored Lawrence and focused her attention on me. "Keegan, you may not remember me, but your mother and I were good friends once upon a time. My, you have grown into a beautiful young woman," she gushed.

I beamed, "Of course, I remember you. What a pleasant surprise seeing you here tonight. Tell me, how have you been?"

She grinned and focused on Lawrence, "My apologies for interrupting, Senator. My excitement at seeing Keegan got the better of my manners. Please excuse us so we may catch up without disrupting your evening any further," she drawled.

She pulled me toward her table, and we spent the rest of the evening catching up and sharing fond memories of my mother. Something over my shoulder caught her attention. She looked at me, winked, and said, "Watch this." I watched in awe as she walked alongside Lawrence toward the front of the building, all the while talking his ear off. Before I knew it, she had gotten him to agree to let me join her for a nightcap. He left with no argument, and suddenly, I found myself staring at the mystery man from the dance floor only to soon learn he was Jacquelyn's son. Mortified didn't even begin to describe how I felt when she caught us kissing in the limousine, but to be frank, I was also seriously disappointed at the interruption. Never in my life had I been kissed like that, with such passion and need. I didn't have a lot of experience with men, but I was no virgin either. Maybe it was his mysterious persona that made the kiss feel electric.

Jacquelyn didn't allow any discomfort to take root. She joked with her son about catching him in the backseat of a car with a girl and then continued talking as if nothing had happened. Jacob sat silently, but I could tell he was listening intently to the conversation I was having with his mother.

"I see no reason to keep up the formalities now that we are in familiar company," she said with a wink. "So, tell me, is Lawrence still the pompous jack ass he was when he married your mother?"

I gasped, "You didn't like Lawrence?"

"I hope I haven't offended you, dear, but no, I most certainly did not like him. I tried to talk your mother out of marrying him. I've often wondered if that's the real reason we drifted apart," she mused.

"No, you haven't offended me in the slightest. I can't stand the man, but I have to tolerate him in order to see Gabriella. If I do something he doesn't like, or don't do something he has ordered me to do, he won't let me see her," I said, not intending to blurt out my business to a woman I hadn't seen in years. Although, she felt like family more than anyone had since Mom's death, with the exception of Gabriella.

"I see. What sorts of things does Lawrence ask of you?" she asked gently.

"Tonight's a prime example. He insisted that I attend the charity ball, more or less as Preston Hensley's date," I said, noticing how Jacob seemed to shift uncomfortably when I mentioned Preston.

"And you're not interested in the Hensley boy?" she asked, grinning mischievously.

I wrinkled my nose, "Not in the slightest. Lawrence is pushing for me to date him, and I don't want to, but I'll have to play along until I figure something out, or he gets bored with this plan and moves on to something else."

"Tell me, dear, are you still living at home?"

I shook my head, "I haven't been back to live

there since I left for college when I was 17 years old. "

She tapped her index finger against her chin, "Hmmm. Seems odd for him to try and marry you off when you aren't a burden to him or his household."

Surprise washed over my face. "I didn't— How did—" I sputtered.

She smiled sadly, "I know how these things work, dear. The only reason he would push for you to date someone in particular is because he wants it to end in a marriage, but you already knew that, didn't you?"

I nodded and fought back the tears. "Yes," I rasped.

She wrapped her arms around me, "Oh, sweet girl. All will be okay. I will help you figure this out." Her words had the tears I was fighting falling down my cheeks. "Keegan, has anything else happened that I need to know about?" I looked at her with panic in my eyes. "It won't leave this car. I just need to know what we are dealing with," she promised.

"H-he, he's sometimes violent...with me," I whispered through my tears. I chanced a glance at Jacob. He was sitting ramrod straight with his fist balled by his sides. He looked a lot like the men from Blackwings at that moment.

"Oh, honey. He won't be doing that again. I promise," she said vehemently.

When we arrived at her estate, she promptly called Lawrence and told him we passed several accidents along the way, and in the interest of my safety, she would prefer for me to stay the night in her guest room. She was good at handling him. I made a note to ask for lessons. Once finished, she showed me to the guest room and provided me with something to sleep in—a red, silky negligée with a matching robe. After bidding me goodnight, she left me alone in the decadent guest room.

I took my time with my nightly ablutions before sliding into the luxurious nightgown. Normally, I slept in a tank top and shorty shorts, but I would definitely be purchasing a few silky negligées for myself in the near future.

I audibly groaned when I slid into the bed. The mattress was soft and pillowy yet firm and supportive. Oh yes, Jacquelyn was officially in charge of approving all my future large purchases.

I turned off the bedside lamp and tried to relax. My body was tired, but my mind was working overtime. The moments I spent with

Jacob were playing in my mind over and over again. I wanted to see his face. I wanted to hear his voice. And, more than anything, I wanted to kiss him again.

Somewhere in the state between wakefulness and sleep, I thought I heard a noise, but it didn't concern me enough to investigate. It was probably my mind playing tricks on me. I had been desperately trying to fall asleep, and I was almost there. Then, suddenly, I wasn't. I felt the bed shift beside me and knew that I was no longer alone. My heart rate increased, and I fought to keep my breathing steady and even. For the moment, I wanted the intruder to think I was still asleep.

A warm hand landed on my cheek, causing me to flinch. "Relax, it's just me," Jacob whispered.

Even though I was pissed at him for scaring me, my body did relax. "What are you doing in here?" I asked, stupidly whispering back to him.

He leaned closer, continuing to whisper, "I think you know." Then, he covered my lips with his. My arms wrapped around his broad shoulders, and I moaned into the kiss. He started slow and gentle, gradually deepening the kiss while his hands caressed my body.

He moved his mouth from my lips to my

jaw, kissing down my neck. I tightened my arms around his shoulders and pressed my body to his, eliciting a soft groan from him. Threading my fingers through his hair, I pulled his head away from my body. "Jacob," I whispered. Then, like the hussy I was, I fused my lips with his and used my body to roll him to his back, climbing on top of him.

With my legs straddling him, I kept my mouth on his, enjoying the feel of his soft lips as his tongue thrust in and out of my mouth with an unmistakable rhythm. His hands went to my hips, gripping me firmly. That was when I realized I had been rocking my hips and grinding down on him. I pulled back, utterly embarrassed. At least the darkness kept my face hidden from him.

He fisted my hair and pulled me to him, whispering, "Not that. Not yet." He nipped at my bottom lip before whispering, "Doesn't mean I've had my fill." We proceeded to make out like teenagers before falling asleep in each other's arms.

The sunlight streaming through the large windows woke me. The smile on my face vanished when I rolled to the side and realized I was alone. It shouldn't matter. It was just a kiss. Okay, a lot of kisses, but I thought we had some sort of connection. Suddenly, I felt like a fool. I didn't know what he looked like; I hadn't even heard his voice. So why was I so disappointed when I woke up alone?

After using the bathroom and brushing my teeth, I realized I had nothing suitable to wear. As if I had conjured her myself, Jacquelyn softly knocked on the door before peeking her head around the corner. "Good morning, dear. I come bearing gifts." She held up a garment bag before placing it on the bed. "I thought you might need something to wear to breakfast with Lawrence. We'll leave in 20 minutes." She laughed at my obvious confusion. "Didn't I mention it? I'm joining you for breakfast." With a whirl of designer fabrics, she left the room.

CHAPTER EIGHT

Shaker

A week had passed since I crept into the guest room at my mother's house and broke a number of my personal rules. Even worse, I couldn't stop thinking about her. Her eyes, her lips, the way she moaned and gasped with pleasure. The softness of her skin under my palm. The penetrating gaze of her startling blue eyes. The blind trust she gave to me.

I couldn't stop thinking about her, yet I wouldn't go to her even though I knew where to find her. She knew me as the mysterious Jacob Marks, not the Blackwings brother Shaker. I could have been wrong, but I assumed the realization they were one and the same wouldn't sit well with her. My mother held a different opinion. She had called me every single day since the charity ball trying to convince me to pursue Keegan. Even if I truly wanted to pursue her, I couldn't, and Mom wasn't aware of that. What a clusterfuck. Keegan didn't know Shaker was also Jacob, and Mom didn't know Jacob was Shaker. I should have made my life easier and come clean with both women, but I couldn't bring myself to do it.

Keegan was nothing more than a passing infatuation, which did not entitle her to know my secrets. My mother's world would never collide with mine, so there was no need to divulge any information to her either. The only thing I needed to do was make sure I was never in the presence of my mother and Keegan at the same time, unless I was wearing a mask. Problem solved.

I was sitting at the bar at the clubhouse contemplating another beer when I heard her voice. What was she doing at the fucking clubhouse? "I know he's your brother and you love him, so I'm going to apologize in advance for strangling him," Keegan seethed.

"Girl, you don't have to explain anything to me. I grew up with him. As long as you don't kill him or permanently harm him, have at it. I have no doubt he deserves whatever you dish up," Harper replied.

"It's not worth the trouble," Keegan mumbled, sounding defeated.

"What do you mean?" Harper asked.

"Nothing I say or do is going to change the way he treats me. He made up his mind about me on day one. That's why I turned in my notice this morning. Stupidly, I thought he would back off once he found out I was leaving, but no such luck."

"You what?" Harper and I asked at the same time.

Keegan looked at me curiously, "I turned in my notice this morning. His home is here, mine isn't. The whole reason I moved here was to work at the horse farm so I could get some experience under my belt and hopefully get my own farm up and running one day, but I'm not learning anything new here. Duke micromanages me when I do anything other than muck the stalls. I'm tired of wasting my time."

"Where are you going to go?" Harper asked.

Keegan shrugged, "I don't know yet. Likely, somewhere that is closer to my sister."

I stood and left the clubhouse. Climbing

onto my bike, I peeled out of the forecourt with one destination in mind.

The ride over did nothing to cool my anger. I stomped into the barn and slammed Duke against the wall, pinning him with my forearm across his neck. "What the fuck is your problem with Keegan?"

His eyes widened at my question. "My problem? What the fuck is your problem?"

"You being such an asshat to her is my problem! She's leaving because of you!" I roared. The look of surprise on his face told me he didn't know about her resignation. "She gave her notice this morning."

I shoved away from him and glared. "She came here to learn more about running a horse farm because she wants to have her own farm one day, but you couldn't be bothered with her. That's not the kind of man I thought you were, brother."

He held up his hands, "Look, man, I didn't know any of that. Keegan and I have different backgrounds with horses. She was always questioning my techniques and telling me how they did things on her stepfather's farm, like she thought I knew fuck all about this business."

"Did you ever stop to think that she was

asking questions so she could learn? That maybe she was telling you about her experiences so you could explain to her if those methods were the best approach? No, you didn't. You saw her as a pretty, little rich girl who was trying to undermine you."

He looked to the floor and sighed, "I'll talk to her."

"No," I growled, "you won't."

I left the barn without another word and headed to my next destination. I found Ember in her office. She was on the phone, but gestured for me to have a seat when she spotted me hovering in her doorway. She finished her call and gave me a curious look, "What's shakin', Shaker?"

I nervously shared my idea with her. If she shot me down, I could still put my plan into action, but it would mean sharing things about myself I wasn't ready to share. I laid everything out for Ember and quietly waited while she seemed to mull it over. She sat back in her chair and scrutinized my face. "If you lose your infatuation with Keegan, are you going to march in here and demand I pull the plug on this?"

I choked, literally choked on my own spit. "Uh, no," I sputtered. "This has nothing to do with an infatuation with Keegan. It has more to do with Harper," I lied. "They've become close, and I don't want Harper to lose her friend."

She tapped her pen on her desk, "You and I both know that's a load of crap, but I'm willing to overlook it because I do think this is a good idea. The money we could bring in from this will be more than enough to fund the animal therapy program Harper wants to start. Give me one second," she said and reached for her phone.

I tried to school my face into a mask of indifference and waited patiently while she made her phone call. After a few sentences, I realized she had called Phoenix to get his approval to move forward with her plans. When she ended the call, she was smiling brightly. "Let's make it happen. Do you want to give Keegan the good news?"

"No, no. You can handle that," I said. "I would prefer to keep my name out of it if you don't mind."

***

It had been two days since I went to the farm to confront Duke and talk to Ember. Two days and I hadn't heard a word about Keegan. Did she accept the offer? Was she staying in Croftridge?

"You want some company?" one of the new club whores murmured in my ear while trying to slide into my lap.

Shoving her away, I told her how it was. "You're new here so maybe no one told you, but I don't fuck with club whores. At. All. I don't want your pussy, I don't want your ass, and I don't want your mouth. I won't tell you again." She glared at me as she slithered away. Like I gave a shit if I offended her.

"What's the matter, Shaker? Not interested in the new girl?" Reese asked, taking a seat beside me.

I took a long pull from my beer before answering her, "Not at all. What are you doing here?"

"Tomorrow is my day to clean, and let me just tell you how much it sucks to clean up after a party. The place usually looks like, well, like an MC clubhouse the morning after a wild party. I'm trying to prevent that from happening," she snickered.

I shook my head. Reese was always getting herself into trouble, which was exactly why she was cleaning the clubhouse in the first place. "What are you up to now?"

She grinned, "Watch and learn."

We continued to chat until Ranger walked by our table. Reese stopped him and asked if he was going to the bar. When he said yes, she smiled sweetly, "Would you mind grabbing a beer for me? Oh, and since you're going that way, could you drop these empties in the trash?" Ranger grabbed the empty bottles, winked at Reese, and continued to the bar.

Reese smiled proudly, "I plan to move from table to table and do that all night. The drunker they get, the easier it'll be."

I threw my head back and laughed. The girl was clever. "You're an evil little genius."

"What's so funny?" Harper asked, joining our table.

"Reese's attempt to get out of cleaning the clubhouse after a party," I blurted.

"Hey! That is not what I'm doing," she said, feigning offense. "I'm trying to lighten the load. What are you doing here, Harper? I thought you had plans with Keegan tonight."

"I did, but she called and canceled, so I came by to see my man," Harper said, wiggling her eyebrows.

"Stop right there before you violate the terms of our agreement," Reese shrieked, covering her ears with her hands.

"Why did Keegan cancel?" I asked, trying to sound nonchalant.

Harper shrugged, "I don't know. She sent a text saying something came up that she had to deal with."

I downed the rest of my beer and excused myself from the table. After dropping an armload of empty bottles in the trashcan, I took quick strides to my room. Her text could have meant anything, but the dread pooling in my gut had me thinking it was something significant. I decided it wouldn't hurt to ride by her house and see if anything was going on.

I managed to slip through the back door and reach my bike without being seen. If the girls spotted me leaving, I would have been bombarded with questions. I was well aware both Ember and Harper thought I was into Keegan. And they weren't wrong. I was into Keegan, really into Keegan, and that scared the hell out of me. I gave my whole heart to a girl one time, and she shattered it. Not long after, I gave a piece of myself to another girl, and, again, she destroyed it. So, yeah, I was into Keegan, but I didn't have anything left to give her.

When I pulled onto Keegan's street, I noticed the lights in her house were on, and a car was parked in her driveway. The sight of the ostentatious sedan had my hackles rising. I climbed off my bike and didn't even bother knocking since her door was slightly ajar. I didn't hesitate to push it open and let myself in. And, I saw red.

CHAPTER NINE

Keegan

After turning in my resignation, things did not go as I had expected. Ember tried to talk me out of leaving at first, but ultimately said she understood when she realized I wasn't going to change my mind. Later the very same day, Ember asked me to come to her office. When I arrived, she told me she wanted to expand her current farm to include raising and training thoroughbreds, and she wanted me to run it.

I sat in her office with my jaw hanging open, unable to formulate a response. "Don't look so surprised," she giggled. "I'm always looking for ways to expand our current business ventures. I told you earlier today you're a valued employee, and I didn't want to lose you. This way I don't have to...if you accept that is."

"This sounds like a dream come true for me, but I'll be honest, I'm not sure I'm qualified to run it," I admitted. "I do have experience as a rider and as a trainer, and I have a Bachelor's Degree in Equine Science, but I've never been the one to oversee the entire operation."

"Don't worry about that. I'll find a consultant to come in and show you the ropes. I won't let you fail," she said, her blue eyes full of hope.

"Okay," I murmured. "I'll give it a try."

Ember squealed and rounded her desk to hug me. "This is going to be great. I'm so excited!"

I smiled genuinely, "I am, too."

The next day, I was scheduled to work at the barn. I arrived on time and was shocked to find Duke waiting for me in the office. I glanced at my watch to double check the time making sure I wasn't late. "Do you have a minute?" he asked.

"You're the boss, you tell me," I retorted.

"I owe you an apology. A big one," he stated. I could only stare at him. "I've misjudged you and treated you poorly from the first day you arrived. When you asked questions and talked about your previous experiences, I took that as you questioning my capabilities. It never occurred to me that you were trying to learn. I don't have an excuse for my behavior, but I am truly sorry. If you're still interested, I'll be happy to answer your questions and share what I know," he said.

I was flabbergasted. The giant asshole known as Duke was apologizing and offering to help me. I narrowed my eyes, "How did you figure out I was trying to learn?"

He looked to the ground and kicked at the dirt with the toe of his boot. "Let's just say it was brought to my attention and leave it at that."

"Ooookay." I was unsure of what to say to him at that point.

"So, are you still interested in trying to gain some useful knowledge?" he asked.

"Might as well," I shrugged.

That day and the next were like working with a completely different person. Duke was a wealth of knowledge. For the first time since I started working at the barn, I was not looking forward to my days off. Duke promised to pick up where we left off the next day we worked together. At the end of the second day, I thanked him repeatedly before finally getting into my car and driving home. Harper and I had plans, and I was desperately in need of some girl time.

I showered and got myself ready to meet Harper. We were planning to do some shopping and then have a late dinner. I was putting the finishing touches on my makeup when I heard someone knocking on the front door. Assuming it was Harper, I yelled for her to come in. Once I finished in the bathroom, I walked into the living room and stopped dead in my tracks.

"Hello, Keegan," an unwelcomed voice said.

"What are you doing here?" I asked, stunned to see Preston Hensley in my living room.

"I wanted to see you, and we need to discuss a few things. Have a seat," he stated, gesturing to *my* couch.

"You should've called before driving all the way down here. I have plans with a friend tonight."

"Cancel them," he ordered. When I opened my mouth to protest, he added, "I'm not leaving. We are having this discussion tonight. Call and cancel your plans."

Maybe it was the tone of his voice or the darkness in his eyes, but something told me not to argue with him. I sent a text to Harper canceling our plans and warily took a seat on the couch. "My plans have been canceled. What do you want?"

"I know you are aware of our impending nuptials. While in public, we should have a proper courtship, but I see no reason to maintain that façade in private, especially after I learned of your association with a motorcycle gang," he sneered.

"I'm not following," I said, a sense of unease unfurling.

He scoffed, "I did not wish to spell it out for you, but you are leaving me no choice. I see no reason to wait until we have said our vows. If you can spread your legs for a bunch of gang bangers, you can spread them for me, too." Before I could respond, his hand shot out and wrapped around my throat. Squeezing tightly, he used his hold on my neck to position me on my back on the couch.

I clawed at his wrist, kicked my legs, shoved at his chest, anything I could to try and get him away from me. "That's right. Fight me," he purred in my ear. I didn't know what to do. My instinct told me to keep fighting him, to protect myself by any means necessary, but if I couldn't fight him off, I didn't want to make his violation more enjoyable for him. His free hand slid up my shirt and roughly squeezed my breast, causing me to freeze. This wasn't happening. Couldn't be happening.

He pawed at my body while he ran his open mouth over my cheek, ear, and jaw, leaving a trail of his disgusting saliva behind. Tears streamed down my face as he reached for the button of my jeans. My will to fight kicked in again, and I began thrashing beneath him. He groaned and pressed his hips between my legs. I could feel the bile rising in my throat, and I started to panic. I was going to die choking on my own vomit while this bastard raped me in my own damn house. I could barely breathe, and my vision was getting fuzzier by the second.

Suddenly, the hand around my neck was gone, and his crushing weight disappeared. My head was spinning, and my vision was blurring in and out. I could hear loud noises followed by groans, but I was too weak to raise my head and look. I curled into a ball and tried to concentrate on breathing. I was well on my way from having my air supply cut off to hyperventilating.

A hand landed on my shoulder causing me to jerk away and let out a yelp. "Keegan," a familiar voice called. "Open your eyes. Please."

The desperate plea had me cracking my eyes open just enough to make out the person crouched in front of me. Shaker. Before I could think about what I was doing, I launched myself into his arms and sobbed. He held me tightly, rocking back and forth while murmuring soothing words into my hair for long minutes.

When I finally had myself somewhat composed, I raised my head, and my eyes immediately landed on Preston's bloodied body lying motionless on the floor. I gasped, "Is he dead?"

Shaker snorted derisively. "No, the fucker's still breathing."

I turned back to Shaker. He didn't have a single mark or scratch on him. And then something occurred to me. "What are you doing here?"

"I'll explain later. Did he, did he, um—," he stumbled. I knew what he was trying to ask.

"No, he didn't, but he would have if you hadn't stopped him," I told him. Then, barely above a whisper, I added, "Thank you."

A small nod was his only acknowledgment of my gratitude. "Do you want the club to handle this, or do you want to report it to the police?" he asked.

I chewed on my bottom lip while I thought about his question. I would much rather the club handle it, but Preston was affiliated with rich and powerful people, and I didn't want the club to get into any trouble. On the other hand, Preston was affiliated with rich and powerful people and would likely get out of any charges against him, especially if he was affiliated with Lawrence. We weren't in Kentucky though, so maybe it wouldn't be as easy for Lawrence to sweep it under the rug. For my own sake, I needed to try handling the situation the correct way. If that didn't work, I would explore other avenues.

"I think we should let the police handle it," I said softly.

He nodded and made the call.

Several hours later, Preston had been arrested, Shaker and I had given statements, and the police finally left my house. All I wanted to do was take a shower, put on my most comfortable pair of pajamas, and crawl into bed.

"I don't think you should stay here tonight," Shaker said. "Let me take you to the clubhouse, at least for tonight."

I didn't have the energy to argue with him, and honestly, I didn't want to stay at my house. Preston hadn't broken in or anything like that. I had unknowingly told him to enter my home, but I still felt creeped out just from standing in the living room. "Okay. I need to grab a few things, and I'll be ready to go," I agreed.

He looked shocked but didn't comment. When I was packed and ready, he locked up the house and led me to his bike. Without a word, I climbed on behind him and wrapped my arms around his waist. He pulled onto the road, and I laid my head against his back, breathing him in. I didn't know Shaker very well, but there was something familiar about him. I briefly wondered if I was losing my mind. First, I thought there was something familiar about Jacob and now Shaker. Clearly, I had an underlying issue with males that was choosing now to surface.

When we arrived at the clubhouse, he led me through the back door to another door that opened into a quaint bedroom. "You can sleep in here tonight," he said.

"Whose room is this?" I asked, partially wondering if I should request new sheets for the bed.

"Mine."

"Where are you going to sleep?"

"If you want me to stay, I can sleep on the floor or in the chair. If you would rather be alone, I'll go home and crash."

"What were you doing at my house?" I asked

again.

He sighed and ran his hand down his face, "I overheard Harper telling Reese that you had to cancel your plans because you had to deal with something that came up. As soon as she said that, I knew something was wrong and rode straight to your house."

"But how did you know something was wrong?" I asked.

"Because I'm not the person you think I am," he blurted.

"What?" I shrieked and started to back away from him.

"That came out wrong. I am Shaker." He paused for a beat before meeting my eyes, "But my given name is Jacob Kingsley Marks."

CHAPTER TEN

Shaker

"Get out," she ordered, her tone eerily calm.

"Let me explain," I insisted. "Then, if you still want me to go, I will."

If looks could kill, I would have dropped dead on the spot. She crossed her arms over her chest, making the top curve of her plump tits visible. I tried not to look, I really did, but my eyes paused there before lifting and locking with hers. "You have five minutes. And keep your eyes on my face, asshole," she spat.

Fair enough. I exhaled slowly and began, "I didn't set out to intentionally deceive you. I thought you were safe because you agreed to stay away from your stepfather. Then, Harper told me he was insisting that you attend the charity ball, and you were planning to go. Harper said she was worried about you, and frankly, so was I. I called my mother and asked her to have me added to the guest list. My only intention was to watch over you and make sure you were safe. I had planned to stay out of sight, even after I found out it was a masquerade ball. When I finally spotted them, I hovered near Senator Hastings and the Hensleys, eavesdropping on their conversations when I could. But, when Preston walked up and said you were in the ladies' room, I decided to check on you since I hadn't seen you all night. I didn't expect to find you in the hall fighting back tears. I also didn't expect the sight of you to steal my breath away. I probably should apologize to you, but I'm not going to because I'm not sorry for dancing with you, and I'm not sorry for kissing you."

I paused to gather my thoughts. I wanted to explain my current behavior without delving into anything from my past. "I'm not going to explain the how or why, but I didn't tell you who I was because my mother doesn't know that I'm involved with the Blackwings, and I don't want her to know. On that note, no one in the club knows that I am, as you put it, 'the never seen, never heard from' son of Jacob and Jacquelyn Marks. That's not who I am anymore, and I don't want to risk them treating me differently if they found out I could buy everything in this town and still have plenty of money left over."

"None of that explains what you were doing at my house tonight," she muttered.

I shrugged, "Call it intuition if you want. I just knew something was wrong. I figured it wouldn't hurt anything to ride by your house. When I saw the car parked in your driveway," I shook my head and cast my eyes to my boots, "I knew Senator Hastings wouldn't have driven himself to your house, but I had a bad feeling. I was going to knock when I noticed your door wasn't closed, and then I heard what sounded like a struggle. So, I pushed the door open. You know what happened after that."

She kept her eyes on me and remained silent long enough for it to become uncomfortable. "How long have you known who I was?"

"I had no idea you were Hastings's stepdaughter until the day I came to return your wallet," I said. "Before you ask, I didn't know that our mothers were friends either."

She nodded, still staring at me with her

arms crossed. I took that for what it was and sighed, "I'll let you get some rest. I'll be back in the morning."

I moved forward to pass her so I could get to the door. I was right beside her when she whispered, "Don't go."

I stopped and turned my head toward her, searching her eyes, "Are you sure?"

"Yeah, I'm sure. I'm tired, and I need to sleep. We can talk about this more tomorrow," she said with a yawn. I moved toward the chair in the corner of my room, preparing myself for a night of little to no sleep when she added, "We're both adults. Sleep in the bed and keep your hands to yourself."

I climbed into the bed beside her, keeping as much distance between our bodies as I could considering the size of the bed. I was by no means the biggest brother in the club, but I wasn't what anyone would consider a small man either. Keegan was average height for a girl, and she had a small frame, so we were able to sleep on my queen-sized bed while respecting each other's personal space. She rolled to her side with her back toward me. Within a few minutes, I heard her breathing even out and knew she had fallen asleep.

I tossed and turned for hours before drifting off to sleep. I couldn't get my mind off Keegan. I felt drawn to her in a way I had never felt before, not even with Beth, and that scared me. The pain I felt from Beth's betrayal almost destroyed me. What would it feel like if I let Keegan in and she did the same thing or something even worse? I couldn't take that chance. As much as I wanted to, I couldn't let anything happen between us. We could be friends, but nothing more.

I woke the next morning to find Keegan wrapped around my body. Her head was resting on my chest, with one arm slung over my stomach, and one leg intertwined with mine. And I was hard as a rock. Fuck! That was when I realized I had one of her tight ass cheeks in my hand and a perky tit cupped in the other. I immediately removed my hands from her body and started trying to extricate myself from the bed when she rolled her hips forward and let out a soft moan. Fuck me. What had I done to deserve such torture? Was this some sort of test of my willpower? Because seriously, I was going to fail and fail epically.

"Keegan," I called, my voice gruff and raspy from sleep. "Wake up."

"Mmm, Jacob...please," she moaned, rocking

those damn hips of hers again.

I couldn't take much more of this. "Keegan," I barked loudly.

She jolted and sat upright with wild eyes darting around the room. When her eyes landed on me, her cheeks flushed. She tried to maintain her composure, but she couldn't hide her embarrassment from me. "What the hell, Shaker?"

"Need to piss. You were on top of me," I grunted and quickly got out of bed. Her eyes fell to my hard cock. I shrugged, "Morning wood." Then I bolted from the room like the bitch I was. I had to get away from Keegan Kensington and get myself together.

Strolling into the bathroom, I figured a cold shower was the only way I was going to get my dick under control. Well, I could have rubbed one out, but with Keegan on the other side of the door, I didn't want to take the chance of her overhearing.

Distractedly, I reached for my body wash while I rinsed the shampoo from my hair. But, when I tried to flip the lid, it wouldn't open. Confused, I looked at the bottle in my hand and immediately cursed when shampoo ran into my eyes.

"Shaker? You okay?" Keegan called out as she knocked on the thankfully locked bathroom door.

"All good," I answered and continued to rub my stinging eyes.

Finally, the burn faded, and I looked down at the bottle in my hand. The bottle that was not my normal body wash. No, I was holding something called Penis Cleaner. What in the actual fuck? I put that shit back and finished my shower with my regular body wash.

Once dressed, I grabbed my phone from the nightstand and stepped out into the hall to make a call, leaving a confused looking Keegan sitting on my bed.

"It's a little early, brother," Carbon grumbled down the line.

I pulled the phone from my ear and glanced at the time. "Sorry, man, didn't even think about that."

"What's up?" he asked through a yawn.

"I saw Harper cleaning the bathrooms earlier this week. Ask her if she's the one who put Penis Cleaner in my shower."

I heard Carbon suck in a breath and maybe stifle a laugh. "You're on speaker. Ask her yourself."

"Two words, Harper. Penis. Cleaner," I said.

"Oh," she said cheerfully. "Do you like it?"

So, it was her. I cleared my throat. "Uh, Carbon, brother, you want to take this one?"

The fucker laughed. "Nope, it's all you, bro."

"What are you two talking about?" Harper asked innocently.

I groaned. "What do you think Penis Cleaner is, Harper?"

She giggled, "Penis cleaner."

"Okay, yes, but it's not soap. It's a spray, that can be used without water. Like on-the-go. Now, why would a man need to use something like that?" I asked, hoping she was understanding what I wasn't saying.

It took all of five seconds. She gasped, and I heard a distinct slap, followed by a grunt from Carbon. "You're telling me I bought a case of dirty dick spray for the clubhouse?" she screeched.

"Why'd you hit me? I didn't have anything to do with this," Carbon said defensively.

"Because you're the only man around right now," Harper huffed.

"Hold up. You bought a case of this shit?" I asked.

"Yeah, I put one in each of the bathrooms," she said, sounding embarrassed. "I thought it was like special soap for guys. You know, like girls have for their lady bits to help with shaving and stuff."

I couldn't help it. I laughed until I was doubled over in the hall gasping for breath. Finally, I got myself under control and wiped the tears from my eyes. That's when I realized she'd hung up on me. Still chuckling to myself, I headed for the common room only to crack up again when Reese ran by me with her phone pressed to her ear and three bottles of Penis Cleaner in her arms as she darted into one of the rooms.

I got some breakfast and sat at a table by myself in the common room hoping to resolve some of my inner turmoil. I liked Keegan, a lot, but the thought of being in a relationship with any woman made my skin crawl. Okay, so maybe the thought of being in a relationship with Keegan didn't make my skin crawl, but it should, and it greatly troubled me that it didn't.

Keegan also had her own shit to deal with. Her stepfather and the Hensleys were up to something and weren't beyond using physical violence to achieve it. I suspected there would be some backlash from the incident last night. Keegan had wanted to do the right thing and let the police handle Preston. I didn't understand why she bothered. Lawrence would pull some strings, call in some favors, and Preston's charges would magically disappear.

To put a stop to her problems, we needed to find out what Lawrence's plans were. Then, we could figure out how to stop them. That would take some time, and she would be left vulnerable in the interim. I felt an overwhelming need to protect her and much to my chagrin, I had only come up with one way to immediately ensure her safety and thwart the senator's plans.

"May I join you?" Keegan's soft voice interrupted my thoughts.

I looked up to see her standing beside the table holding a plate of food. I nodded and kicked a chair out with my foot. She sat and began eating her meal in silence. Neither of us spoke. I was too consumed with the ridiculousness of what I was about to suggest.

When we were both finished, she asked, "Can I go home today?"

"I don't think that's a good idea. I'm sure your stepfather, as well as the Hensleys, are going to be pissed when they find out what happened to Preston last night." I leaned forward, placing my folded arms on the table, "Why was Preston at your house in the first place?"

She sighed and slumped in her chair. "As you know, Lawrence has arranged for me and Preston to be married soon. Preston somehow found out that I have ties to the Blackwings and said if I was fucking a bunch of bikers, I could fuck him, too."

I growled low in my chest. "Who are you fucking?"

She rolled her eyes and scoffed, "No one, unless my vibrator counts."

I peered at her and licked my lips. "That doesn't count."

She met my gaze and held it, "Don't I know it."

She was killing me. Death by blue balls would be listed as the cause on my death certificate. My mind was screaming "no," and my dick was screaming "yes, please." I blatantly adjusted my cock and groaned, "You have to stop."

The little vixen winked, "Whatever do you mean?"

"Focus, Keegan. What are you going to do about Lawrence? He's not going to give up. Are you actually planning on marrying Preston?"

"No, I'm not planning on marrying him! I haven't had time to find a way out of this," she stated.

"Do you know why he wants you married?" I asked. There was a reason behind this marriage. I all but heard as much in the men's room at the masquerade ball.

"No. The only thing he told me was that he was tired of my behavior, and it would be my husband's responsibility to deal with it if I were married," she shrugged.

"What behavior?"

She shrugged again, "Your guess is as good as mine. The only thing I've missed was a late brunch the day you found me on the side of the road. Other than that, I've not failed to meet any of his demands."

I took in a deep breath and went for it. "Listen, this is going to sound crazy, because it is, but I know how we can put a stop to this." I paused and locked eyes with her. "We should get married," I blurted.

She blinked, and her expression remained unchanged. She didn't give me any kind of reaction. "Did you hear me?"

"I'm sorry," she said slowly. "I think I just had a mini-stroke. You were saying?"

"Keegan, I'm serious. Lawrence can't force you to marry Preston if you're already married. I'm not suggesting we get married for real, just on paper."

"Getting married on paper is for real," she deadpanned.

"Yes, it is, but we don't have to stay married. As long as we don't consummate the marriage, we can get it annulled after we've figured out what Lawrence is up to. It will buy us the time to do that and keep you safe. As my wife, you'd have the club's protection," I explained.

"You're serious?"

I nodded, "I don't see any other way to make him back off."

Her eyes started to fill with tears, and her lower lip trembled, "He won't let me see Gabriella if I marry you."

"I'll be honest with you. You might not be able to see each other for a few months or however long it takes to put an end to this. I know Lawrence made a deal with the Hensleys which included your marriage to Preston. We need to find out what the rest of that agreement was and why they made it in the first place. I have a feeling you can use that information as leverage to see your sister," I explained.

She sniffled and wiped the tears from her cheeks. "Okay, I'll do it."

CHAPTER ELEVEN

Keegan

Shaker didn't think we should waste any time. After a quick internet search, we found a location, made a reservation, and purchased a wedding package online. He had his clothes and toiletries at the clubhouse, but I needed to stop by my house to get a few things. I packed a small backpack with my necessities and climbed onto the back of his bike to go get married.

We headed to a popular tourist town about an hour and a half from Croftridge. It was a cute little town packed full of attractions, as well as wedding chapels. They even had a courthouse open on Saturdays to issue marriage licenses.

We were in and out of the courthouse with the necessary paperwork in less than 10 minutes.

"We have almost two hours before our reservation. Are you hungry?" Shaker asked.

I wasn't hungry. I was scared and nervous and too worked up to even think about food. "Not really, but if you're hungry, you should eat."

Shaker nodded and drove to a pancake house. He caught me eyeing him and shrugged, "You can't come to this town and not stop for pancakes."

Shaker insisted that I order something and try to eat even though I assured him I was fine. We sat in silence while I picked at my food, and he didn't hesitate to inhale his order. When he finished, he wiped his mouth with a napkin and leaned forward on his elbows, "What's wrong? You have cold feet or something?"

Cold? My feet were fucking frozen. "I guess I'm a little nervous," I admitted. "What if this doesn't work?"

"How can it not? You can't marry Preston if you're married to me. Besides, the senator might be thrilled to hear his stepdaughter married into the Marks family. I am quite a catch, you know," he said, flashing me a toothy smile.

"What will your mother say?" I whispered.

Our elopement would definitely upset Jacquelyn.

"Would you feel better if we told her the truth?" he asked.

"Yes. A lot better. She'll keep it to herself?"

He chuckled, "She will. In case you haven't noticed, my mother is not a fan of Senator Hastings." He glanced at his phone. "It's about that time. You ready?"

I laughed nervously, "Not in the slightest."

The wedding chapel we chose offered an all-inclusive package for spur of the moment elopers. Basically, all we had to do was show up with a marriage license. They took care of everything else, including a dress for the bride and a tuxedo for the groom. Initially, I assumed we would have a courthouse wedding, but Shaker thought the story would be more believable if we had photographic evidence of our extremely private ceremony when we made the announcement. I hadn't even thought of making a formal announcement. As Shaker pointed out, it was what would be expected of us unless we wanted everyone to think I was pregnant. Enough. Said.

An older woman introduced herself as Rose, my wedding attendant, and escorted me to the bridal suite. She showed me their large selection of wedding dresses and left me alone to choose one. When she returned to find me staring at the row of dresses with tears running down my face, she pulled me in for a hug and asked, "How long ago did you lose her?"

I couldn't hide my shock. "Five years. How did you know?"

She smiled softly, "I've been in the wedding business for a long time, dear. I know the look of a bride missing her mother. Don't you worry about a thing, sweetheart. I know just the dress for you."

Rose knew what she was doing, and she could do it all—dress, hair, makeup, nails. By the time she finished with me, I looked like I stepped off the page of a bridal magazine. I couldn't thank her enough. She managed to comfort me and turn me into a princess in less than an hour.

She led me to a set of closed doors and told me it was go time when the doors opened. I could feel the panic rising within. Before it could take hold, the doors swung open, and there was Shaker, standing by the altar waiting for me. In a tuxedo. Looking like the illegitimate child of sex and sin.

I don't remember walking down the aisle. One second, I was staring at the closed doors contemplating running away, and the next, I was beside Shaker. Then, I was facing him, staring into his obsidian eyes. I was transfixed by the sheer presence of him, my gaze never leaving his, until one sentence broke the spell.

"May I have the rings, please."

The rings. We didn't have rings. We had to have rings. How could wedding rings have slipped my mind? Oh, because you don't think about things like that when you're planning a fake wedding in less than thirty minutes.

Shaker winked and reached into his pocket. He opened his closed fist and dropped something in the minister's hand. Then, the minister was handing something to me—a ring—and instructing me to repeat after him. He did the same with Shaker. I gasped when Shaker slid not one, but two rings onto my finger—an engagement ring and a band. Correction, a humongous, breathtakingly gorgeous engagement ring and a diamond wedding band. I looked from the rings to Shaker and back again. He gave me a subtle shake of his head as the minister prattled on. Then, another sentence caught my attention.

"You may now kiss the bride."

I had to kiss Shaker. We'd kissed before, but that was different. He was wearing a mask the first time, and it was in total darkness the next time. And I didn't know it was Shaker. We should have discussed the kissing part beforehand.

Shaker stepped forward, cupped my cheeks with his hands, and softly pressed his lips to mine. He deepened the kiss, coaxing my mouth open and sliding his tongue inside. His hands held me in place while he kissed me with the same passion I received from Jacob, but never expected from Shaker. When he finally pulled away, I would have crumpled to the floor had he not been holding me. He winked and smiled slyly, "Come on, wifey, it's time for the honeymoon."

Surely, he was joking, right?

CHAPTER TWELVE

Shaker

The look of shock on Keegan's face was comical. Being the asshole that I was, I didn't tell her I was kidding. Actually, I didn't say anything else to her until we arrived at the clubhouse. She seemed to be just as lost in her thoughts as I was.

I took her in through the back door since there was no doubt a party was going on in the common room. Once in my room, I said, "I'm going to call my mother and fill her in on our nuptials. As far as the club goes, I don't want to lie to my brothers, but we can't have too many people knowing the truth. We're going to have to act like husband and wife, which means we'll have to live together. So, your house or mine?"

"Is my house safe? If you're not there?" she asked.

"If you want us to live in your house, I'll have a prospect keep watch whenever you're home alone."

"Okay. I want to live in my house," she said. "Thank you for doing this for me. And for remembering the rings. I'll make sure to take good care of them until I give them back to you."

I shrugged, "You don't have to give them back. You can keep them." I didn't want the rings back. I didn't want to see them on Keegan's finger either. She was wearing the rings I bought for Beth before I found out she was a gold-digging, cheating, whore. It seemed fitting to use them for a fake marriage.

"I'm going to go ahead and call Mom," I stated, pulling out my phone and effectively stopping any protest from her.

My mother took the news better than I expected. Surprisingly, she thought it was a great idea and offered to help in any way she could. I expected to be chastised for tarnishing the sanctity of marriage and intentionally deceiving virtually everyone we knew. Instead, she commended me on my clever thinking and told me how proud of me she was for trying to keep Keegan safe. Then, she insisted on hosting a wedding reception and demanded I send her a wedding photo to use for the announcements. With a promise to do just that, I ended the call.

"We have to send her a photo for the announcements, and she is going to host a wedding reception in the near future. Now, we need to tell Phoenix," I said.

"The truth?" she asked.

"Yes. I don't like lying to my brothers, but I will not lie to Prez. He may want to share the truth with the other officers. I'm okay with them knowing, but there's no reason for the entire club to know," I replied.

We slipped into the common room unnoticed. I spotted Phoenix immediately and asked if I could have a word with him in private. He grumbled under his breath and started walking toward his office. Keegan and I followed him inside.

"Why is it there's usually trouble whenever you two are together?" he asked.

"Sorry, Prez, I don't think this time is going to be any different," I offered. I told him everything, only leaving out the few times we had kissed. "The only other person who knows the truth is my mother, and she will keep it to herself. I don't like keeping things from the other brothers, but for this to work, people have to think we are really married. I have no doubt the senator could manage to get the marriage annulled if he were to find out the truth."

Phoenix nodded, "I understand, and I appreciate you telling me. I would have stripped you of your title and maybe even your cut if you'd kept this from me. I think the other officers should be made aware. I'm sure Keegan's stepfather and the supposed fiancé won't be happy to hear your news. It'll be good to have a few more people keeping an eye out for suspicious activity. You gonna claim her as your Old Lady?"

"I wasn't sure if I would be disrespecting the club if I did," I uttered. It would be odd if a brother married a woman and didn't claim her as his Old Lady. It wasn't unheard of, but it would raise some questions.

"It would have been if you hadn't come to me. If you think you should claim her, I'll allow it," Phoenix said.

"Then, yes, I want to claim her as my Old Lady," I stated firmly.

"No time like the present. Most everybody is here tonight," Phoenix said, standing and gesturing toward the door.

Fuck! I was hoping for a few days before I had to make any kind of announcement or declaration to the club. I reached for Keegan's hand and tugged her along with me. "Smile, wifey. It's show time."

We entered the common room, and Phoenix shut off the loud music to get everyone's attention. I cleared my throat, "This is going to come as a shock to many of you." I raised our clasped hands in the air and shouted, "Keegan and I got married today. She's now my wife and Old Lady."

Silence.

Keegan yanked her hand from mine and burrowed into my side, "Shaker, why aren't they saying anything?"

I wrapped my arm around her and pulled her closer, tipping my head down to murmur in her ear, "Don't know, sweetheart, but everything will be okay."

"Holy shit! You're serious?" Duke blurted.

"Wouldn't joke about something like this, brother," I snapped.

Suddenly, we were swarmed by brothers and Old Ladies congratulating us and offering well wishes. I knew we could pull this off. I was only worried about one person. Harper. We'd become close during and after our kidnapping and she was also good friends with Keegan. If anyone was going to doubt our sudden marriage, it was going to be her.

Harper was the last to approach us, looking at both of us with an appraising eye. "Congratulations! I hope everything works out for you." She hugged us both and went back to sit with Carbon.

"That was odd," Keegan whispered.

"Yeah, it was. We'll have to be careful around her. I think she already suspects something is off," I whispered back. I leaned in closer to her, keeping my voice a whisper, "We need to act like newlyweds. You going to be okay with that?"

She swallowed audibly. "It's fine. It's not like we haven't kissed before," she said with a wink. Then, she stood on her toes and placed her lips on mine. Instinctively, I wrapped my arms around her waist and pulled her closer, deepening the kiss for a few beats. I pulled back and grinned, "I bet that looked believable."

She playfully smacked my chest, "You're shameless, Shaker Marks."

We spent the rest of the evening at the party, laughing and drinking with our friends. Keegan stayed by my side or in my lap for the majority of the night. I couldn't say that I didn't enjoy having her next to me. I could, however, say that I didn't like enjoying the feel of her body pressed close to mine. She was a friend I was helping. Nothing more. I would not allow this damsel in distress to seduce me only to destroy me later.

With my newfound determination, I told the ones remaining we were going to bed. That got a variety of responses from the rowdy group. Once in my room, I told Keegan I would see her in the morning. She gaped at me and looked like she wanted to say something, but she just nodded and told me goodnight.

I slipped through the back door and climbed on my bike. I needed some distance from her and sleeping in the same bed was not the way to get it. I drove around for a while and thought about riding out to Cedar Valley and finding a girl to take back to my fuck pad, but I couldn't do it. It just seemed inherently wrong to fuck someone other than my wife on our wedding night, even if the marriage was a farce. Ultimately, I went to my apartment in Croftridge and crashed.

The following morning, I went back to the clubhouse to pick up Keegan. I checked my room, but she wasn't there. She wasn't in the common room, the kitchen, or out by the pool.

She couldn't have left because she didn't have her car and I knew she wouldn't have asked anyone for a ride and risked blowing our story. I flopped down on a couch by one of the pool tables and tipped my head back.

That's when I heard it. Laughter. Feminine laughter. Keegan's laughter. Followed by male laughter. Oh. Hell. No.

Jumping to my feet, I stomped down the hall, following the sounds of more laughter and giggling. When I found where it was coming from, I pushed the door open and froze at the sight before me. Keegan was in Byte's bed. With Byte. They were side by side and laughing hysterically.

"What the fuck is going on in here?" I roared.

Keegan snapped, "What the fuck does it look like?"

"It looks like my wife is in bed with my brother the day after our wedding!" I shouted.

She looked down at herself, over to Byte, and back to me. "I would say that's correct," she sneered.

Byte held his hands up, "Whoa. I'm going to stop this before it goes any further. We were sharing some of our computer secrets at breakfast. I told her about some of the games I play when I'm bored. We came back in here to reset the screensavers on the computers at the fire department."

"You what?" I asked.

"We changed the screensavers to say stuff like, 'I burn for you' or 'You light my fire,' stuff like that," he explained, causing Keegan to start giggling again.

She braced her stomach with one arm and said, "The best one was 'Firemen have big hoses. Spray me hot stuff.'"

The corner of my mouth twitched. I didn't want to laugh, but that shit was funny. I knew Byte would occasionally play pranks on the folks of Croftridge, but I had no idea what he specifically did. "Sorry, brother. I didn't mean any disrespect by having your Old Lady in my room. I guess it slipped my mind because it's so new."

"It's fine, brother. I trust you...and her. I was worried when I couldn't find her, and it shocked me to find her in your bed," I explained. I turned my eyes to Keegan, "Let's go."

She jumped to her feet and stomped toward me, "Yes, boss."

I followed her to my room and closed the door. "What is your problem?"

"My problem?" she screeched. "My problem

is spending my 'wedding night' alone while my husband was filling a cum bucket at his fuck pad in Cedar Valley! That is my fucking problem!"

I chuckled, "Sounds like somebody is jealous."

Her face scrunched and turned a bright shade of red. "I most certainly am not jealous. What I am is disgusted. Did it even occur to you that someone might have seen you? Or perhaps the slut you were with might talk? I don't give a shit what you do, but I do not wish to be publicly humiliated in front of people I will have to face long after you have come and gone."

"Whatever you say, sweetheart. Just so you know, I slept at my apartment in Croftridge last night, alone. I didn't go anywhere else, not that it's any of your business. Your turn, how did you know about my place in Cedar Valley?"

She held up both hands and wiggled her fingers, "I'm good with computers. I was bored last night and couldn't sleep, so I ran a few checks on you. I figured I should know more about you now that you're my husband."

Not a big deal. So, she knew about my fuck pad. She didn't know what I did, or didn't, do there. As long as I kept my dick in my pants for the next few weeks, there was no way she could find out about my particular issues. I tried to feign nonchalance, "Learn anything exciting from your checks? Aside from the fuck pad, that is."

She grinned, "I did. You, sir, should have insisted upon a prenup."

I threw my head back and laughed, "You can't be serious."

"Obviously, it's too late for a prenup, but I do think we should sign a postnuptial agreement as soon as possible. I would never try to take your money from you, but neither one of us knows what kind of stunts Lawrence might try to pull. I would feel better if I knew your rightful assets were protected," she explained.

She didn't want my money. She wanted to make sure no one could take it from me because of her. I didn't know what to do with that information. I had been screwed over before by a beautiful woman. Was she playing some sort of trick on me? Trying to lull me into a false sense of security. Before I could think better of it, I blurted, "What would you do if you got pregnant?"

Her eyes widened, and I heard a small gasp. "That won't happen. We agreed not to consummate so we could get it annulled."

"Humor me. Say you did get pregnant, what would you do?" I insisted.

"I'm not sure what you're asking. If I got pregnant with your baby, I would have it and raise it. I wouldn't expect you to stay married to me just because we had a kid together. I would hope that you would want to be a part of the child's life though," she said.

"What about money?" I asked, not liking the hint of urgency in my tone.

"What about it? I have a good job and enough from my trust fund to live comfortably and raise a child on my own. I wouldn't refuse financial support for the child if you offered, but I wouldn't take you to court for it. Whatever you contributed, I would spend on the child and put the excess in an account for them," she explained. "Why? Do you want to include a section about potential children in the postnuptial agreement?"

I was struggling to come up with a plausible reason for my questions. As she answered each one, she unknowingly provided me with an excuse. "Yes, I think we should. It would look suspicious if we didn't. I'll get in touch with my mother's lawyer first thing Monday morning."

CHAPTER THIRTEEN

Keegan

The following Wednesday, I was stepping out of the shower after work when there was a knock on my bedroom door. I wrapped a towel around my hair and another around my body before opening the door. Shaker stood there slack-jawed, not bothering to hide his obvious perusal of my exposed skin. I cleared my throat to get his attention, "Did you need something?"

"Uh, yeah. I have a copy of the postnuptial agreement. After we review it, if we don't have any changes, we can sign it and have it notarized and mail it back to the lawyer," he said to my chest.

"I'll get dressed and be right out," I said and closed the door. I didn't understand Shaker sometimes. He was obviously attracted to me and cared about my safety and well-being, but whenever anything happened between us, he would push me away. I wondered if his actions had anything to do with his kidnapping. He never mentioned it when he was around me, but it must have had some kind of effect on him. Maybe I could talk to Harper about it.

We ordered some food for delivery and reviewed the document while we ate. It was relatively simple once translated from convoluted lawyer speak. Basically, we would each keep what we had prior to the marriage. Any inheritance after the marriage would belong solely to the heir. I would keep my house. We would each keep any income earned and savings generated. In terms of finances and assets, it would be as if we were never married.

The section on potential children gave me pause. It was more detailed than any other portion of the agreement. After reading the entire section, it dawned on me—it was a custody agreement. In order to get the marriage annulled, we couldn't consummate, so there was no chance of pregnancy. Still, it seemed odd to me that so much detail was included in this type of agreement. It even included a section on abortion.

"Doesn't this seem like a lot of detail for a child that hasn't even been created yet?" I asked.

He paused, his forkful of food in midair, and shifted in his seat. His eyes didn't meet mine when he said, "I have no idea. It's not like I've done this before. I asked for a standard 'you keep your stuff and I keep mine' postnuptial agreement, and that's what they sent."

He seemed defensive. I shrugged, "I was just curious. It doesn't really apply to us since you have to have sex to get pregnant. I don't have a problem with anything in the agreement. Do you?"

"No, I'm good with it. I'll call Patch when we're finished eating and see if he's available to notarize it for us. I want to get it back to the lawyer as soon as possible," he said.

Later that evening, Patch stopped by my house, our house, and notarized our agreement. I saw him give Shaker a quizzical look, but he didn't comment. He was in and out within a few minutes, leaving Shaker and me alone in the house. Something had shifted between us, and I was unsure of what to do with myself. "I'm going to head to bed. Today was busy, and I'm worn out," I told him.

"Oh, our wedding announcement will be in the papers this weekend. Mom included the information for the reception she's hosting, which will be two weeks from Saturday. Make sure you stay vigilant; Lawrence will no doubt be pissed when he finds out," Shaker said.

I was so out of my element with this entire situation. Should we register somewhere? I didn't want people buying gifts for our fake marriage, even if they could afford it. It didn't seem right. Should we invite our friends from Croftridge? It would be rude if we didn't, but Shaker said his mother didn't know about his affiliation with Blackwings MC. I was beginning to feel overwhelmed. I went back to the kitchen and poured myself a glass of wine before curling up in bed with my e-reader. I would worry over the details another day.

***

I had to work the rest of the week through Saturday. Sunday was my only day off until the Friday before the reception. As expected, my phone started blowing up not long after the sun came up. I ignored it and stumbled to the kitchen for coffee. I rounded the corner and froze. Shaker was standing in front of the coffee maker, his back to me, wearing nothing but a pair of loose drawstring pants. If he turned around, I feared I might melt into a puddle of goo on the floor.

I silently backed away and dashed for my room. I quickly brushed my teeth, washed my face, and ran a brush through my hair. I changed from my ratty t-shirt and oversized sweatpants into a form-fitting tank top and yoga pants. Feeling much better about my appearance, I ventured to the kitchen once again to find Shaker still in front of the coffee maker. Facing me.

Holy.

Shit.

My eyes immediately landed on his chiseled chest and slowly slid down to the delectable V exposed by his pants hanging low on his hips. I glanced at the bulge between his legs and then let my eyes slowly make their way back to the top. When I got to his face, I was met with a knowing smirk, "You done eye-fucking me?"

I shrugged, "Maybe. If you don't like it, put a shirt on."

His lips twitched. "You cold?" he asked and tipped his head toward my chest.

Motherfucker! I should have put on a bra. My traitorous nipples looked like they were trying to poke through my thin tank top to get to Shaker. I shrugged again, desperately trying to mask my embarrassment with indifference, "I can appreciate a nice male specimen when I see one. Doesn't mean I'm going to hop on and ride him to town. Now move, I need coffee."

He pushed off the counter and slapped my ass when he passed, "Whatever you say, wifey."

I ignored him and poured myself some coffee. Sighing, I sat at the kitchen table and began to look at the missed calls and messages. Almost all were from Lawrence. I rested my forehead in my hands and tried to prepare myself for the ass-chewing I was sure to receive.

My phone buzzed on the table. Before I could answer it, I felt a warm hand on the back of my neck and heard Shaker's deep voice say, "Good Morning, Senator Hastings, or should I call you Dad?" Good job, Shaker, poke the already pissed off bear.

I could hear Lawrence's angry voice, but I couldn't make out what he was saying. "No, sir, you may not speak to my wife. I do not care for your tone and do not wish to subject her to it. As I am her husband, anything you need to say to her can be said to me."

More stern words from Lawrence. I looked to Shaker, worry evident on my face. He winked, "Senator Hastings, I would like to remind you of whom you are speaking with before you continue on with your tirade. I have no problem sharing your tendency to verbally abuse my wife with my family's friends, many of which I do believe are large contributors to charities you support as well as your own campaign. It would be a shame to lose a large portion of your funding simply because you cannot control your mouth."

There was a pause. When Lawrence spoke again, his voice was noticeably quieter. "Oh, that's much better. See, it's not hard to be civil. Oh, one more thing worth mentioning; this call is being recorded. In fact, I'll take this opportunity to inform you that any and all calls in the future will also be recorded. Now then, would you still like to speak to Keegan? To offer your congratulations?" Shaker was silent for a few beats. "I assumed not. Good day, Senator Hastings."

What the hell was that? I was in awe of my husband and the way he put my asshole stepfather in his place. I stood and turned to face Shaker, "That was amazing. Thank you."

"Let me know if you hear from Preston or the Hensleys. I can take care of them, too," he said.

I promised I would, kissed him on the cheek, and went back to my room in hopes of going back to sleep. After an hour of trying, I gave up and took a shower. With it being my only day off before the reception, I needed to find something to wear. I called Harper and invited her to join me. Once I was ready, I picked her up, and we headed to Cedar Valley to do some power shopping.

I still wasn't sure if we should invite our friends from Croftridge, and I hadn't talked to Shaker about it. I couldn't very well tell Harper we were shopping for a dress for my wedding reception that she wasn't invited to, so I told her I had a formal event to attend. Not a lie, but not the complete truth either. I felt horrible deceiving so many people. I hoped they would understand it was for my safety when it was all over.

We were in the dressing room of the fourth or fifth store we had been to when she asked, "So, you and Shaker, huh? How did that happen?"

"Uh, I don't know. We hit it off, and, on a whim, we decided to get married," I said, stumbling over my lie.

"He's a good guy. I didn't know him very well

before we were both kidnapped, but we developed some sort of bond through the ordeal, and now I consider him to be one of my good friends," she said.

"Since you mentioned it, do you know what happened to him? He has mentioned it in passing, but he never talks about it in any detail," I said carefully.

She sighed, "No, I don't know the details of what happened to him. I've tried to get him to talk about it, even urged him to seek counseling, but he always refuses. I know he was taken two days before I was, as a sort of test run in preparation for taking me." She paused and lowered her voice, "I'm only telling you this because you are his wife. Please don't mention it to anyone else, and please, please don't tell him I shared any of this with you." When I gave her my word, she continued, "When I was trying to get out of the house, I heard him yelling for help. I didn't know anyone else was in the house, but he knew I was there. He was locked in a room on another floor. I unlocked the door to find him handcuffed to a bed, completely naked. He had bruises and scratches all over his body. I undid his cuffs, and we got out of there as fast as we could. I don't know if you knew this or not, but the girl who kidnapped us was the daughter of the man who kidnapped me when I was a child. She was posing as my best friend and coworker...and she had also been seeing Shaker for several weeks before the kidnapping."

"The girl he was with at the wedding, right?" I asked, remembering not liking her on sight.

"Yeah, she went by Hilarie, but her real name was Valarie."

"She was his girlfriend, and she kidnapped him?" I asked.

"I wouldn't say she was his girlfriend," she said hesitantly. She cleared her throat, "They were fucking, not dating." That pissed me off. He could stick his cock in that psycho bitch, but he ran screaming for the hills every time he kissed me.

This whole mess was confusing. I knew it was best if we weren't together like that, especially while we were faking a marriage, but I wanted him to want me. Because I wanted him even if I didn't want to admit it.

"I see. Well, I've found a dress. I just need to find some shoes, and I'm finished," I said, hoping to change the subject. I did not want to hear any more about Shaker and his whore.

"What about jewelry?" she asked. Subject

change successful!

"I have a set at home that will go perfectly with this dress. I probably have shoes that will work, too, but who in their right mind passes up an opportunity to buy a new pair of shoes?" I asked, eliciting a giggle from Harper.

While I was paying for the dress, I noticed a man standing outside of the store looking in our direction. I probably wouldn't have seen him if it hadn't been for his bright red hair. I focused on the cashier while I completed my transaction. When I glanced back, the man was gone. I couldn't put my finger on it, but something about that man made me feel uneasy.

I knew something was off when I saw the man standing outside of the shoe store. I will say he was well hidden, but I was specifically looking for him as I hid behind a row of shoes. Upon seeing his bright red hair again, I called Shaker.

"I think someone is following Harper and me," I whispered into the phone.

"Where are you? Where's Kellan?" he barked.

"We're at the mall in Cedar Valley. Who's Kellan?" I answered.

"A prospect. He's your shadow today. I meant it when I said I would have someone on you when I wasn't with you. Stay in the store until you hear from Kellan or me," he said before disconnecting. Was the redheaded guy Kellan? Shaker should have introduced me to the man he had following me.

I heard Harper's happy voice, "Kellan! What are you doing here?"

I took that as my cue to join them. I wasn't sure if I was happy that Kellan wasn't the man with the red hair or not. While it would have explained why he was following us, the redheaded man gave me the creeps. I approached the two of them and held out my hand, "You must be Kellan. I'm Keegan Kensington, I mean Marks. Keegan Marks. I haven't gotten used to the name change yet," I said, laughing nervously.

Kellan smiled kindly. He was the very definition of a boy-man. "Everything okay?" another boy-man asked, appearing out of nowhere behind Kellan.

"Yeah, man. They're good," Kellan answered.

"Coal?" I asked, surprised. "What are you doing here?"

Coal chuckled, "Kellan asked if I wanted to tag along. Sometimes shadowing is less, well, boring, if you do it in pairs."

I felt my cheeks heat. "I'm sorry you have to

follow me. If I'd known, I wouldn't have taken so long to choose a dress. I'll just grab some shoes, and we can go."

"No need to apologize. It's my job. I think what Coal meant was it's easier to stay focused when you're with another brother. It's easy to zone out and get lost in thought when you're sitting or standing by yourself," Kellan explained.

Coal and Kellan escorted us from the store to my car. I looked for the redheaded man the entire way to the car, never once spotting him. The boy-men followed us on their bikes back to Harper's place and then to mine. It wasn't until I pulled into my driveway that I realized I never heard back from Shaker.

CHAPTER FOURTEEN

Shaker

Kellan would be getting my vote when it came time to patch him in. He had been a prospect for almost a year, and he was damn good at it. He had asked Coal and Edge to tag along with him while he tailed Harper and Keegan. When Keegan called me and said she was being followed, I immediately called Kellan. He was headed into the store as we spoke. He'd noticed the man well before Keegan ever did. With Coal and Edge there, they were able to nab the guy, and the girls were none the wiser.

Edge was a good brother, too. He had followed Coal and Kellan in a cage. A few months ago, Edge told me he had learned from his previous experiences with the club it was better to have a cage handy than to have to wait for one if a situation arrived. I knew he was referring to the time when Coal was shot and almost died. Edge shoved the man in the cage and brought him back to the clubhouse while Coal and Kellan followed the girls home.

I stood in front of the man tied to the chair and snarled with disgust. I didn't have to ask who he was or what he was doing. I knew he was hired by the senator to follow Keegan. What I didn't know was how far the senator was willing to take this. Was this guy just a PI trying to get information, or was he one of the senator's goons sent to hurt Keegan?

"Do you know who I am?" I asked. He nodded. "Tell me. Who do you think I am?" I wanted to see how much he knew. I wasn't in the habit of volunteering information to people I didn't know. No one in the club was.

"You're Jacob Kingsley Marks. You're also Shaker, Road Captain for Blackwings MC," he sputtered.

"Sounds like you did your research. So, you know exactly what kind of position you've gotten yourself into?" I asked.

He shook his head, his whole body starting

to tremble in fear. "N-no, I don't. I didn't know you were part of a biker gang until I saw your cut. I read your road name and position off your patches."

"Club. It is a motorcycle club. Why is that so hard for people to get?" I asked rhetorically, shaking my head. "Let me bring you up to speed. You were tailing my wife. The girl with her, she's the little sister of our SAA, and she's our enforcer's Old Lady."

I heard the door open behind me. "Fuck me! You made him piss himself before I got here," Carbon chuckled briefly before his eyes darkened. He focused his ice-cold stare on the man while directing his question to me, "Did he scare my woman?"

"Nope. She has no clue this douchebag was following them," I answered.

Carbon's face changed to an almost pout, "I never want my woman scared, but I was looking forward to making him pay for it."

"Start talking," I barked at the scared ginger.

"Um... S-senator H-hastings hired me to follow his stepdaughter. He said she was mixed up with a biker gang, his words, not mine, and he wanted me to report everything back to him— where she went, who she was with, what she ate, everything," he blurted.

"Yes or no," I said, giving him a warning look. "Did he say anything about me?"

"No."

"How did you know who I was?" I asked, hoping his answer wouldn't do more harm than good.

"You don't recognize me?" he asked, surprised.

"Should I?" I spat.

"We met once, years ago. I'm Bernie, Beth's cousin," he said shakily. "I didn't know you were any part of this until just now. I swear it. Hastings told me Keegan had recently married, but he didn't tell me who she married."

"When did he hire you?"

"Yesterday," Bernie shakily answered.

"Fuck me!" I grunted. Was this a random coincidence, or did Senator Hastings hire this prick from my past on purpose? "Well, Bernie, we have ourselves a little problem here. I can't just let you go. You know too much. I don't really think it's fair to kill you since you didn't know what the senator was signing you up for," I said, pausing to let it sink in. "So, here's what's going to happen. You are going to tell us everything you know about the senator and everything he's said to you. Then, I'll decide if Carbon here gets to play with you."

He squeaked and fervently nodded his head. "I'll tell you whatever you want to know." And he did. He talked for over an hour. Unfortunately, the senator was a smart man, and not much of the information was helpful. Most of what he said only confirmed what I already suspected. The senator was not happy about Keegan's marriage. He wanted the PI to find something that he could use to end the marriage or something he could use to blackmail one of us. That little tidbit got my attention, but I didn't share that with Bernie.

"Please don't kill me," Bernie whined.

I studied him while I pretended to contemplate his fate. "What are you willing to do to convince me to let you live?" I asked.

"Anything. I'll do anything," he swore.

"Sit tight," I chuckled and nodded my head toward the stairs. Carbon silently followed me to Phoenix's office. Apparently, he was still pouting.

I brought Phoenix up to speed, leaving out the details of how Bernie knew me. Then, I explained my idea. If it went wrong, it could easily be denied. If it went as planned, it could possibly provide us with a solution to the problem. Phoenix mulled it over and ultimately agreed.

I returned to the basement. Bernie was still trembling in his chair. When he heard me approaching, his head shot up with wide, panicked eyes. "If you agree to three things, I'll let you go. One, you will not say a word to anyone about being at our clubhouse today. Two, I will tell you what to report back to the senator. You will tell him nothing else. Three, you will give said report at the senator's house and plant a bug for us while you're there. What do you say, Bernie?"

He looked at me skeptically. "That's all I have to do to leave here unharmed?"

"We're not monsters, Bernie, contrary to what a lot of people think. But don't let that fool you, we will hunt you down and make you suffer if you don't follow my instructions. Do you understand?" I asked.

"Yes, I understand. I won't say a word to anyone, I promise," he blubbered.

We went over the information he was supposed to give the senator. He was to tell Lawrence it appeared as though I was head over heels in love with Keegan, that I would do anything for her. I wanted Hastings to focus on me instead of Keegan. In the meantime, if Bernie could plant the bug in his home office, we would be listening for a way to get him out of Keegan's life for good.

"You think he'll keep up his end of the deal?" Carbon asked me while we were having a drink at the bar in the common room.

"Yeah, I do. Bernie's a good guy. Not the smartest, but he means well. He probably rushed down here thinking he was on a mission to save Keegan from a bunch of brutal bikers," I said. "I highly doubt he had any clue the senator was up to no good."

I got back to Keegan's house later than I expected. I briefly wondered if I should have called to let her know, but quickly reminded myself that we were not actually married and I didn't have to answer to her. All the lights in the house were off, and it was eerily quiet. Assuming Keegan had already gone to bed, I tried to be quiet while I grabbed something to eat from the fridge. That's when I heard it — a faint moan.

Quietly, I crept toward Keegan's room, to make sure she was okay. Yeah, even I didn't believe that. Her bedroom door was slightly cracked; it was enough for me to see her in bed. With her vibrator. Between her legs. I was a sick bastard because there was no way I was going back to my room and giving her privacy. I watched as she pleasured herself, my cock growing harder by the second. She was going to town with that thing, and it was driving me wild. When she finally climaxed, she whispered my name. Not Shaker. She said Jacob, and the sound of it just about unmanned me.

I backed away from her door as quickly and as quietly as I could. Once I was far enough away to avoid being caught, I bolted for the shower. I had a massive, throbbing issue to tend to.

***

I didn't see Keegan much for the next week. By the time I woke up, she had already left for work, and she was in bed when I got home. Thankfully, she was in bed sleeping and not doing anything else. Surprisingly, I found myself missing her company. Keegan wasn't like most of the other women I knew. She was more like the Old Ladies of Blackwings. I will admit being envious of the relationships my brothers had with their women, but I never thought it was something I could have for myself, because I wasn't willing to risk it.

I was on my way to the clubhouse when I

got a call from Byte. My helmet was equipped with Bluetooth capabilities, but I chose to ignore his call. I needed to get my head straight and focus on the end goal instead of lusting after Keegan and daydreaming about having what my brothers had.

I thought back to my relationship with Beth. I was so in love with her, or at least I thought I was. Was it really love I felt for her or was it a lustful infatuation? She was a beautiful girl, on the outside. On the inside, she was selfish and manipulative. If that baby hadn't been born with obvious Asian features, I don't believe she would have ever told me there was a chance the baby wasn't mine.

Keegan didn't strike me as the type of person who would deceive and manipulate another, especially for the sole purpose of her own gain. What did I know? I was apparently not a great judge of character. In fact, Keegan was currently in the midst of deceiving and manipulating a large group of people. Although, it wasn't her idea and she did express her dislike for the deceit, even insisted on telling the truth to my mother. And she wasn't doing it to benefit herself monetarily or meet some selfish need; she was doing it for her own safety and for her little sister.

I pulled into the forecourt and pushed through the front doors of the clubhouse. I was in a foul mood and had no qualms about everyone knowing it. Stomping my way to Byte's room, I rapped on his door with more force than necessary.

The door swung open to reveal Byte, glaring at me with furrowed brows. "What the fuck, Shaker?"

"You called me. What did you want?" I barked.

He started laughing. Full on belly laughing while I stood in his doorway fuming. "What is so fucking funny, Byte?" I gritted out.

Through his laughter he managed to get out, "She is really getting to you, isn't she? Oh, this is going to be entertaining."

I pushed forward and grabbed him by his shirt. "No one is getting to me. Is that why you called me over here? To laugh in my face?" I growled.

He shoved against my chest, effectively pushing me away from him. "You need to get in the ring and work off some tension, brother," he said, glaring at me with clenched fists.

"The fuck is going on in here?" Phoenix rumbled from behind me.

"Shaker's trying to take his problems out on me, in my own damn room. Ain't happening," Byte answered.

Phoenix stepped past me into Byte's room and turned to face me. "We'll talk in a minute. Sit down and show some respect to the brother trying to help you and your girl," Phoenix ordered.

"Sorry, Prez," I mumbled. I didn't correct him about her being my girl. For all intents and purposes, she was my girl, even though she wasn't.

"I called you both in here to let you know Bernie called about an hour ago. He met with the senator at his home first thing this morning. He was able to plant the bug in his office. I've got the audio feed up and running. I have it set up to record only when there's audio available and to stop recording after five minutes of silence. I'll get an alert on my phone and computer when there's a new recording. The recordings will be saved and backed up in several locations. I'll let you guys know when we have the first one," Byte told us.

"Thanks, brother. Appreciate it. Sorry about earlier. Got a lot on my mind I guess," I offered.

"I noticed. Get your shit worked out, brother, so you're not taking it out on the people trying to help you," he replied.

"Let's chat in my office," Phoenix said to me. I silently followed him down the hall, feeling like I was going to the principal's office.

"Want to tell me what your problem is?" Phoenix asked.

"I would if I knew," I said. "I don't know what has me on edge lately."

Phoenix leaned back in his chair, rubbing his chin like he always did when he was thinking. "Keegan is what has you on edge. I've known you for years and not once have I seen you show any interest in having a relationship with a woman. Even with Hilarie, we all knew she was nothing more than a convenient, steady piece for you. I imagine there's a reason or two from your past that's turned you against relationships," he said. "Now, you're playing house with a beautiful, sweet girl and putting on enough of a show to make everyone around you believe you two are happy newlyweds. It's understandable, kissing and putting your hands all over her in public, then going home and not fucking her. Frankly, I'm shocked it took you this long to start acting like a total prick to everyone in your path."

My jaw wanted to drop, but I willed it to stay closed. I already knew most of what he said, but it seemed to have more impact to hear it from someone else's mouth. "So, you think I should fuck Keegan, and that will make everything all better?" I asked, failing to hide my skepticism.

"Did I say that?" he rumbled. "No, I said that was why you were acting like a prick. Fucking her isn't going to fix anything. She's not the type of girl you can fuck once or twice and walk away from. She's a sweet girl and will be around Croftridge for the foreseeable future. You yourself made sure of that when you pitched that job to Ember." That time my jaw did drop. "I'm not stupid, boy. I've seen the way you look at her when you think no one is looking. You've put yourself on the line for this girl by marrying her and offering her protection. You wouldn't have done that if you didn't have feelings for her in some capacity."

"I do care about her as a friend, but there can never be anything else between us, for many reasons," I explained.

"Such as?" he asked, with a raised brow.

"For one thing, we agreed not to consummate the marriage so we could get it annulled after we take care of Lawrence," I told him. He nodded and gestured for me to keep going. "You said it yourself, I have never expressed an interest in having a serious relationship, and she's not the type of girl to fuck and forget."

"You ever been in a relationship before?" he asked.

"Once," I mumbled.

"Ah, the bitch must have burned you good. Did you love her?" he asked.

I shrugged, "I thought I did at the time, but now I'm not sure. If what I had with her was love, I don't ever want to be in love again."

"Shaker, if it was love, you would have known it, without question. What happened between you and the girl?" he asked gently.

"We were together for about a year when she told me she was pregnant. We planned to get married after the baby was born. I was by her side through the entire pregnancy. When the baby was born, I knew it wasn't mine. I left and never looked back," I said quietly.

"Anything else?" he asked.

"Uh, yeah, but you already know that story," I said and shifted uncomfortably in my seat. "The club whore that claimed she was pregnant and then said she had an abortion a few days later. Turned out she was lying about both. Anyway, I might have been able to move past the first one if the second one didn't happen. But it did, and, after that, I was done with bitches. No more repeats. Then, I stupidly let Hilarie become a repeat. You know how that story ended," I said.

"Have you ever shared those stories with anyone?" he asked. I shook my head, unable to meet his eyes. "Shaker, I'm not going to pretend to know what's best for you, but I think it would be good for you to talk to Keegan. Tell her what happened to you and see how she reacts. She has shared a lot of her personal business with you. Talk to her about your past and talk to her about the kidnapping. You said you care about her as a friend, let her be your friend. Couples who were friends first have some of the strongest and happiest relationships."

"But we're not in a relationship, not really."

Phoenix sighed. "So you've said. I think you're missing my point. Let her be your friend. She's kind and loyal, and she would probably love to be able to do something for you in return for everything you're doing for her."

"Thanks, Prez. I'll think about it."

CHAPTER FIFTEEN

Keegan

I hadn't seen Shaker in almost two weeks. I knew he came home every night as his bike was in the driveway when I left for work in the mornings. I don't know what I expected our fake marriage to be like, but this wasn't it. I couldn't say for sure, but I had a distinct feeling he was avoiding me, and I had no idea why. I didn't have time to worry about it too much. I had been extremely busy at work, learning everything I could from Duke and preparing to get started on the horse farm expansion.

It was time to leave and drive to his mother's house to get ready for the wedding reception, and he wasn't home. I called his cell phone several times and not once did he answer. I wasn't type A about things by any means, but some form of a plan would have been nice. If I waited any longer, I was going to risk being late to my own reception, regardless of where my supposed groom was.

Sighing, I grabbed my bag and climbed into my car. I put the car in reverse and heard the roar of pipes behind me. Shaker signaled for me to wait and ran inside the house. Moments later he emerged with a duffle bag and walked to the driver's side of the car. "What are you doing?" I asked.

"Driving. Slide over," he grumbled. I should have told him to shove it, but I never cared much for driving. Without a word, I slid into the passenger seat and closed my eyes. It wasn't a long drive to his mother's house, but maybe I could get a short nap in.

"You okay?" Shaker asked once we were on the highway.

"I'm fine," I answered curtly. He hadn't been interested in how I was doing for the last two weeks, so why worry about it now?

He cleared his throat, "I haven't had a chance to tell you. The guy following you and Harper at the mall was a private investigator hired by

Lawrence. We convinced him to plant a bug in Lawrence's office and coached him on what to report back to Lawrence. Don't be surprised if Lawrence's behavior is out of character tonight. We're trying to make him believe that I am completely captivated by you. I have no doubt he will try to get close to us in hopes of getting his greedy hands on some of my family's fortune."

"Okay, thanks for the heads up," I replied flatly.

"What's wrong?" he asked, sounding genuinely concerned.

I shifted to my side, facing away from him, "Nothing. I'm just tired. I'm going to try to catch a nap before we get there."

He didn't argue with me and blessedly drove the remainder of the trip in silence. I, however, did not find sleep. Instead, my mind was in overdrive. I was already nervous about the reception. I never cared for being the center of attention and tonight I would be, while I was pretending to be newly married to Jacob Kingsley Marks. As if that wasn't enough, now I knew Lawrence would be there and would likely try to socialize with me. I shuddered when I wondered if the Hensleys would be there, too. This soirée had the makings of a gargantuan disaster.

A hand on my shoulder was gently rocking me. "Keegan, baby, wake up." I blinked my eyes open to find Shaker hovering over me. "We're here," he announced. I guess I did fall asleep after all.

Jacquelyn was waiting for us inside the front door. She threw her arms open wide and pulled us both into a hug. "My son and daughter-in-law! I'm so happy to see you!" She held us in her embrace for several beats before releasing us. "Jacob, you know where everything is. Keegan, come, let me show you where you can get ready for the party this evening."

Jacquelyn led me into a room that looked very much like a small salon. She grinned when she noticed me looking around the room. "This is what I like to call my styling room. With as many events as I attend, it seemed more convenient to have the necessities in my home and have everyone come to me. I have a makeup artist, manicurist, and hairstylist who should be arriving any moment now. You are welcome to use their services. Through the door on the far side of the room is a small area I use for dressing. We can hang your gown in there."

"Yoo-hoo," a new voice called.

"Oh, my girls are here! Come in, dears,"

Jacquelyn said. "Girls, this is my beautiful daughter-in-law, Keegan. Keegan, this is Bianca, Deanna, and Nadine. They have been helping me prepare for events for years. They are by far the best in the business," she said with a smile.

The girls set up their equipment and set to work. Jacquelyn had some champagne sent up, and soon it felt more like a spa day with friends. Jacquelyn was right; the girls were very talented. Deanna curled my hair and swept it off my shoulders into an elegant updo. Bianca accentuated my eyes by applying a heavy smoky eye paired with a nude lip color. Nadine opted for a French manicure with a light coat of sparkle polish over the white tips for my fingernails and a sheer nude for my toes. When they were finished and turned me to face the mirror, I wanted to cry. I looked and felt beautiful, which wasn't something a girl who spent most of her time in a barn experienced often.

"Don't cry, dear, you will mess up my hard work," Bianca said playfully.

"That's right," Jacquelyn chimed in. "No time for tears. We have just enough time to get dressed before we need to leave."

I was suddenly embarrassed about the dress I purchased for the reception. At the time, I wanted something to catch Shaker's attention, to make him want me. Instead, he would see me as immature and desperate.

"Keegan, are you all right, my dear?" Jacquelyn asked.

I swallowed thickly, "I'm sorry, I didn't mean to worry you. I'm fine; I was just suddenly wondering if I chose the right dress. I guess I'm a little nervous."

"I'm sure it's lovely. Let's have a look," she smiled kindly.

I slipped into my dress and prayed she didn't think I looked like a hussy, because I certainly felt like one — a shameless, desperate hussy. Taking a deep breath, I braced myself for Jacquelyn's disapproval and slowly opened the door with my eyes closed.

She gasped, "Oh, Keegan, it's perfect!"

"Really?" I asked, surprised by her reaction. "It's not too..." I trailed off, unable to think of the right word.

"It's perfect, my dear. Go on downstairs while I get changed into my gown," she said, closing the door behind her.

I took one last look at myself in the mirror, picked up my clutch, and slowly descended the grand staircase. Shaker was standing at the bottom; his back turned to me. My heels tapping on the marble floor must have caught his attention. He turned around and took a step back at the sight of me approaching. "Keegan," he whispered.

I froze, unsure of his reaction. His dark eyes slowly took me in from head to toe and back up. "I have no words; none exist that would do you justice." He smiled shyly and extended his hand to help me down the remainder of the stairs.

"Thank you," I said softly.

We waited in silence for Jacquelyn to come down. I tried not to fidget, but my nerves were starting to get the better of me. Shaker placed his hand on the small of my back and leaned in closer, "Relax, everything will be fine."

I turned my head toward him and, in a moment of weakness, pleaded, "Please don't leave me."

His face was so close to mine. I could feel his soft breaths on my cheek. "I won't. I promise," he murmured before gently pressing his lips to mine in a soft kiss.

I started to turn into his body when a throat clearing caught my attention. We both turned to see Jacquelyn smiling brightly, looking like the essence of sophisticated grace. "Shall we?"

The hour drive to the reception venue did nothing to quell my anxiety. I don't think anything short of an elephant tranquilizer could have at that point. As we were pulling up to the venue, Jacquelyn instructed her driver to take us to a back entrance. We were to wait in a private room while the guests arrived. Then, we would enter the ballroom when we were formally announced as Mr. and Mrs. Jacob Kingsley Marks.

Jacob. I had to remember to call him Jacob instead of Shaker tonight. How was I going to remember that? In my mind, Jacob was my mysterious dance partner from the masquerade ball. The man I shared a few kisses with in the dark. Shaker was the man who repeatedly came to my rescue. The man I married. My friend. My friend who I was wildly attracted to. The man I had spent many nights fantasizing about.

"Keegan?" Shaker called from outside the limo, his hand extended toward me.

"Sorry," I mumbled, placing my hand in his.

We were ushered through the backdoor to a small room to wait until it was time for the reception to begin. I carefully sat and immediately began to worry my hands in my lap. I felt Shaker sit beside me, but I didn't raise my eyes to look at him. "Out with it. What has you so worried?"

"I've never liked being the center of attention. I prefer to blend in with the crowd and watch rather than be watched on any given day. Knowing all eyes will be on me while I'm pretending to be your wife, pretending to have a civil relationship with Lawrence, and potentially having to face Preston and/or his parents is almost more than I can handle," I confessed.

He put his arm around my shoulders and pulled me to his chest. "First of all, you are not pretending to be my wife; you are my wife. As far as Lawrence goes, yes, you have to be civil. If you feel like you are about to lash out at him, squeeze my hand or arm twice, and I will redirect the conversation or steal you away for a few minutes." He paused and used his free hand to tilt my face to his, "Preston will not be here tonight. His parents likely will be, but I can promise you he will not."

"What did you do?" I whispered.

Shaker grinned, "I didn't do anything. I heard he ran into some trouble with a 'biker gang' and would be tied up all evening."

I pulled back and playfully swatted his chest, "You didn't?"

"Again, I didn't," he laughed.

"Thank you," I said softly.

He nodded his head once and softly pressed his lips to mine in a chaste kiss. For the second time that evening, a throat clearing garnered our attention.

"It's time," Jacquelyn beamed.

We entered the ballroom to cheers and shouts from our guests. I glanced around the room, in awe of the sheer opulence of the room. Jacquelyn had chosen well and clearly spared no expense on the reception. The room had an old-world look, decorated in creams and golds, lit by magnificent crystal chandeliers. If I hadn't known better, I would have sworn I was standing in the grand ballroom of a palace. "This place is unbelievable," I whispered to Shaker.

Music began to play, and I was led to the dance floor for my first dance with my husband. I felt like I was in a whirlwind, every twist and turn revealing a new surprise. Jacquelyn had planned everything, even the music. I chuckled softly as Shaker began to lead me around the dance floor to *Beauty and the Beast*. "Your mother has quite the sense of humor," I said with a smile.

He smirked, "I picked the song."

I couldn't contain the giggle that escaped me, "Good choice."

When the song ended, I was forced to stand beside a stiff Lawrence while Shaker danced with Jacquelyn. I didn't have any desire to speak to him, much less any clue what to say, but I felt like I should say something. People were watching after all. "I hope our impromptu reception didn't cause much trouble with your schedule. I apologize for any inconvenience we may have caused," I said sweetly.

"Of course not, my child. I was more than happy to clear my evening to celebrate your marriage to the Marks boy," he replied, sounding surprisingly genuine, though I knew he was anything but. He extended his bent elbow to me, "Our turn."

The father-daughter dance had completely slipped my mind. I wanted to find the person responsible for coming up with these wedding traditions and strangle them. Instead, I plastered a fake smile on my face and stiffly allowed Lawrence to lead me in a waltz. Blessedly, Jacquelyn had chosen a short song, and the awkward dance was over quickly.

Since we didn't have a wedding party, Shaker and I were seated together for dinner with Jacquelyn at his side and Lawrence at mine. Once again, I had the privilege of witnessing

Jacquelyn passively put Lawrence in his place when he attempted to scold me for eloping. "Oh, Senator Hastings, don't let your disappointment of missing their nuptials put a damper on celebrating the love and happiness so obviously shared between these two young souls," she said with a broad smile. I shoved a forkful of food into my mouth to keep from outright laughing at the look on Lawrence's face.

After dinner, we had to suffer through far too many hugs and handshakes, most of which were accompanied by superficial congratulations and conversations. I was on the verge of excusing myself to the bathroom when Shaker suddenly pulled me onto the dance floor and wrapped me in his arms. "What are you doing?" I asked.

"Dancing with my beautiful wife," he replied. Then, he leaned in close as if to nuzzle my ear and whispered, "The Hensleys were headed in our direction, and they didn't seem to be happy."

Great. What were they going to do? Make a scene at the wedding reception of the girl who didn't want to marry their abusive son? Preston and I weren't engaged. Hell, we weren't even dating. They had no right to be angry with me. If anyone, they should be upset with Lawrence for promising my hand in marriage without my explicit permission.

Finally, the party started to wind down. We had danced, socialized, and cut the cake. Before I thrust myself back into the throng of guests, many of which were becoming increasingly inebriated, I slipped away to use the restroom. As I was exiting, I heard heated male voices, both I recognized instantly. Quietly, I took a few steps back and partially closed the door.

"I had no idea she fucking knew him! I couldn't possibly have known she was planning to marry him!" Lawrence said harshly.

"It doesn't matter if you knew or not. What are we going to do now? We only have 30 days!" Mr. Hensley said.

"No need to worry. I have something in the works as we speak," Lawrence replied.

"Something in the works? Something in the works isn't good enough. We need a solid plan or—" Mr. Hensley was cut off.

"We had one! Your son is the one who fucked that up. Maybe instead of complaining and whining, you could help me come up with a solution," Lawrence argued.

"It happened on one of your days, not mine," Mr. Hensley retorted sounding farther away.

I heard Lawrence quietly curse followed by

footsteps moving away from me. I waited for a few beats before exiting the restroom and making a beeline for Shaker. I found him chatting with Jacquelyn and a small group of guests. I forced my face into a smile and walked right to his side. Raising to my toes, I pressed a kiss on his cheek and whispered, "We need to talk."

He waited for a break in the conversation, "If you will excuse me, I want to dance with my lovely bride."

On the dance floor, he held my body tightly to his, allowing us the opportunity to talk without being seen or heard. I told him everything I overheard in the hallway between Mr. Hensley and Lawrence. "What do you think they were talking about?"

"I'm not sure, but I think it would be wise to discuss it later, yeah?" he said.

We continued to dance, and before I knew it, they were calling for the last dance. At the end of the song, Shaker dipped me before yanking me back up to meet his lips in a passionate kiss. The crowd erupted in cheers around us. Shaker grabbed my hand and started for the doors. It was then I noticed the guests were lined up and blowing bubbles for us to run through. As we approached the end, the doors were pulled open, and we slid into a waiting limousine.

I laughed excitedly, "I think that was the best part of the night."

He winked, "The night's not over yet."

CHAPTER SIXTEEN

Shaker

I wasn't sure how I was going to keep my hands off of her when we slid into the car after the reception. The night went better than expected, and I found myself enjoying every second Keegan was by my side. When she wasn't, my eyes were searching for her, needing to make sure she was okay.

When we climbed into the car, Keegan sat a few seats away from me. I didn't care for the space she put between us, but I didn't say anything to her or make a move to get closer to her. Once we were settled and on the road, I glanced over to find her fast asleep. Pulling her to my side, I put my arm around her and rested her head on my chest. I enjoyed the feel of her pressed against my body. She was a good woman, nothing like the ones from my past. I wondered what it would be like to have a real relationship with her. Even if I could get over my issues, I couldn't act on my feelings because of our marriage. We couldn't start dating if we were already married, and if we had sex, well that would mean getting divorced so we could date. I snorted at the thought. I had managed to get myself into the most unusual situation.

Shaking my head to myself, I shut down that line of thinking and called Byte to tell him about the conversation Keegan overheard between Lawrence and Hensley. I had a feeling we might get some information from the bug we planted in his office over the next few days.

"Do you want me to see if I can dig up anything on the senator or Hensley while we're waiting?" Byte offered.

"Yeah, brother, if you have time, I'd appreciate it," I said.

Next, I called Coal. He answered on the first ring. "I assume everything went off without a hitch?" I asked.

Coal laughed, "Piece of cake, brother. Fucker damn near pissed himself when we walked into his house. How was your night?"

"Good. No problems, though I think we'll have something to work with after tonight. I'll fill you in when I'm back in town," I said.

When we arrived at my mother's house, I carefully cradled Keegan against my chest and carried her inside. She must have been exhausted. She didn't stir when I carried her upstairs, changed her into her pajamas, and tucked her into bed. I watched her for a few minutes, taking in her beauty before I kissed her forehead and left the room.

The next morning, I had several missed calls and texts from Byte. I didn't bother reading the texts; obviously, it was urgent. He picked up before the first ring ended. "Shaker, got some info for you. When are you going to be back?" Byte asked, sounding worried.

"I was planning on spending the day with my mother, but I can come back now if needed," I said.

"Yeah, I think that would be good," he said and paused before lowering his tone. "Don't let Keegan out of your sight, brother."

"Understood. I'll see you in a few hours," I said and ended the call. Byte's words put me on edge. The only reason I would need to keep my eyes on Keegan is if she was in danger. He must have heard something or found something to make him believe that she was.

Not wanting to waste any more time, I went straight to the room Keegan was staying in. I skipped knocking and barged into her room. She was awake, but I could tell she hadn't been for very long. "We need to get back to Croftridge. We're leaving in 30 minutes," I told her and walked out of her room.

Next, I went in search of my mother. I found her downstairs at the table finishing her breakfast. She took one look at me and asked, "What's wrong, son?"

I sighed and dropped into a chair beside her, "I'm not sure yet. Keegan and I need to head back to Croftridge immediately. I had a friend checking into a few things for me, and he called this morning to tell me he found something."

My mother straightened in her chair and pinned me with her eyes, "Your motorcycle friends will help keep our Keegan safe?"

I blinked stupidly at my mother. I didn't know what to address first. Our Keegan. Motorcycle friends. I decided to ignore the part about Keegan being ours. "You know about the club?" I asked.

"Of course, I do, dear. I'm your mother. I

don't know why you felt the need to hide it from me. I've only ever wanted you to be happy. After what that dreadful girl did to you, for a long time, I worried you would never find happiness. It seemed like you found a version of it with Phoenix Black and his friends," she said, patting my cheek. "I'll have Suzy pack up some breakfast so you can eat on the road."

I sat there stunned. My mother knew about the club. How long had she known? How did she know about Phoenix? Did it matter? No, it didn't. I had foolishly been trying to keep the two very different parts of my life separate, and clearly, I had no reason to.

"I'm ready," Keegan said from behind me.

We said our goodbyes and were on the road sooner than I had expected. Keegan didn't hesitate to tear into the breakfast Mom sent with us. I loved that she wasn't shy about eating in front of me. After we finished, she asked, "Why did we have to leave so early? Did something happen?"

"Byte called this morning and said he had some info for me. He said the sooner I was back, the better. I don't know any more than that," I explained. I debated whether or not to tell her about his concern for her safety, but decided to wait until I heard what he had to say. There was no sense in worrying her for no reason.

When we pulled into the forecourt at the clubhouse, I instructed Keegan to wait in the common room while I went to talk to Byte. Her response was a sarcastic, "Yes, sir."

I found Byte in his room in front of his computer. "What do you have for me, brother?" I asked, taking a seat beside him.

"He was in his office talking to someone on the phone after the party last night. It must have been a landline because his cell phone records didn't show any calls made or received. It didn't even occur to me to consider a landline. Who even has those anymore? I'm trying to get the number to it now. If I can find it, we can put a tap on it and hear both sides of the conversation," he explained.

"I'll ask Keegan if she has it or knows where to get it. What did you hear last night?" I asked.

"He was talking in some kind of code. He said he was in the midst of securing a new financial resource, one with less red tape than the last. He mentioned having 30 days to finalize the deal. Then he reassured whoever he was talking to that he would have the finances and the product ready to go at the designated time, the same location as before. He also apologized for the 'mishap with the original purchase.' I don't know what he is talking about, but I don't have a good feeling about this, brother," Byte said.

"What the hell?" I mumbled.

"I don't know, brother, but I have a distinct feeling they weren't talking about anything legit..." Byte trailed off.

Yeah, I didn't think they were talking about anything legit either. "Me, too. Thanks, brother."

"Let me know if you can get a number for the office from Keegan," Byte reminded me.

"She's here. Hang on, I'll go ask her," I said.

"She said she didn't even know he had an office in the home, much less a phone number for it. What about Bernie?" I suggested.

"Already checked with him. He only had a cell phone number," he replied.

"Thanks, brother. I appreciate your help," I mumbled, turning to leave.

"Keep an eye on her, yeah? This isn't sitting well with me," Byte said. His concern was out of character for him. He was typically the last one to be overly worried about anything.

I went back to the common room to get Keegan and take her home only to realize she was in the middle of what appeared to be an intense game of pool with Ranger. When I came out to ask her about the phone number, I assumed she was keeping him company while he played by himself, which he did almost every day.

I stood back and watched as they went back and forth with jabs between shots. Ranger was by far the best at pool in the clubhouse, which is why none of the brothers would play him. But Keegan was giving him a run for his money. When she won the game, Ranger was not having it. That turned into a rematch, which led to them playing for the best two out of three, then three out of five. I was going to draw the line at best five out of seven, but they agreed to part ways on a three to three tie.

"Where did you learn to play pool like that?" I asked on the way back to her house.

She giggled, "Promise you won't tell Ranger?" I gave her my word. "I've never actually played before."

"Say again?"

"I've watched other people play, but today was my first time playing." She smiled widely, "It's a fun game."

"You've never played before, and you tied with Ranger?" I asked in disbelief.

"Is that a big deal or something?" she asked.

"Hell, yes, it's a big deal. That man is the best of the best. He used to hustle for large amounts of money. Then, he started playing in tournaments. And he usually won," I explained.

She clapped her hands together and bounced in her seat, "I've always wanted to have a hidden talent!"

I couldn't help but laugh at her child-like response. "You have to let me tell Ranger. He'll want to help you develop your raw talent."

"We'll see," she hedged.

We spent the afternoon opening the gifts from our wedding reception. Though we weren't planning on using any of the gifts as we would be returning them when the marriage was annulled, Keegan thought opening presents of any kind was fun, even the ones she couldn't keep. She made a list of who sent what as she tore into package after package. By the time she finished, we were sitting in the floor surrounded by a sea of wrapping paper, tissue, and empty gift bags.

"This is going to cost a fortune in postage," she said flatly and burst into laughter seconds later.

I smiled and chuckled, "You're probably right about that."

When she pushed up to stand, her foot slid on a piece of tissue paper. Her feet slipped backwards while her body went forward, causing her to crash land on top of me, sending me to my back on her kitchen floor. On instinct, I protectively circled my arms around her and held her tightly to me. Her stunned face was mere centimeters from mine. Before I could give it any thought, I rolled us and put her back to the floor with my legs wedged between hers. Then, I smashed my lips to hers in a bruising kiss.

Her lips parted, and her tongue dueled with mine as her hands clutched my shoulders. With my weight braced on my forearm beside her head, my other hand moved to the juncture between her legs, pressing and rubbing over her jeans.

"Jacob," she breathed. "We have to stop."

I was beyond worked up and not thinking clearly. With my chest heaving, I pushed back so I could see her eyes, "Why?"

"Because we won't be able to get an annulment," she panted, blinking up at me with her beautifully flushed cheeks.

I cursed. She was right, but I decidedly did not want to stop. My dick was throbbing, and my balls felt like they were about to explode.

Gritting my teeth, I rose to my feet and extended my hand to help her up. She sat up and shook her head. Without another word, she shifted to her knees and reached for my belt.

I should have stopped her. I should have known better. But I didn't. I let her release my belt and undo my pants. When she reached for my cock, my reality shifted, and everything changed. My inadvertent self-conditioning kicked in like muscle memory.

I grabbed her wrist and yanked her to her feet. "That's not how this works," I growled and spun her around. Using some ribbon from one of the wedding gifts, I quickly secured her hands behind her back. Then, I turned her back to face me and pushed her to her knees.

I freed myself from my pants and grabbed a fistful of her hair. "Open," I demanded.

She didn't hesitate in the slightest. Those pretty lips parted, and she leaned forward to lick my piercing.

And I lost what little bit of control I had.

I held her head steady by her hair and shoved my cock to the back of her throat. I relished in the warm heat and tight suction of her mouth for a few seconds before I pulled back and began thrusting. I pumped myself in and out of her mouth over and over without pause, taking what I needed from her.

Minutes later, when my balls tightened, and my cock swelled, I pushed forward until I felt her nose touch my skin and shot my load down her throat. And it was more than I'd come in a long time.

When my cock stopped pulsing, I took in a deep breath as I stepped back and looked down to see her tear-streaked face. And that's when reality came back and slapped me in the face.

"Keegan. Fuck!" I barked. What the fuck had I done?

She flinched back and looked up at me with fear in her eyes, causing my jaw to clench. Instead of comforting her or trying to explain my fucked-up-ness, I freed her hands and walked out the door.

***

Almost a week had passed since our rendezvous in the kitchen, and I went out of my way to avoid Keegan, making sure to come home after I knew she would be asleep. I wasn't ready to face her, nor did I have any idea what to say to her. Though, there were no words to excuse what I'd done.

Needless to say, when I walked into Byte's room for an update, I was shocked to find Keegan and Byte, side by side, two sets of wild eyes focused on glowing screens while their hands rapidly flew across their keyboards. "The fuck is going on in here?" I growled.

"Shhh!" they hissed simultaneously.

They stopped typing but were still staring at their screens. Then, I heard several shouts coming from the common room, followed by the sound of stomping boots. Byte and Keegan erupted into peals of laughter, but their laughter died instantly at the report of two gunshots filled the air.

Byte and Keegan rose and started toward the door. I let Byte pass, but blocked Keegan. No way was she going anywhere near gunfire if I could help it. With my gun in my hand, I pushed her back into Byte's room and closed the door. "No, it's not what you think. Let me out!" she screeched.

"No fucking way, Keegan! Did you not hear the gunshots?" I barked.

"Did you not hear me say it's not what you think?" she growled. The little minx growled at me.

Before I could reply, Byte burst into the room carrying mangled pieces of...something in his hands. Keegan looked at whatever Byte was holding and shook her head, "Who shot it?"

Byte grinned, "Kellan and Carbon."

Keegan cursed. "I'll get my purse."

"One of you tell me what in the hell is going on right the fuck now," I demanded.

"We made a robot and dressed it up as one of the munchkins from *The Wizard of Oz*, zombie style. I wanted to make it walk into the common room and scare the crap out of people. Byte said they would shoot it. We made a bet. Then, we bet on who would shoot it, if it was indeed shot. I said Duke and Phoenix. He said Carbon and Kellan. I owe him $50," Keegan explained.

Did I hear her correctly? I didn't care; I wasn't asking her to repeat whatever the fuck she just said. "Why are you here in the first place?' I asked.

She placed a hand on her hip and pointedly informed me, "Because it is a free country, and I can go wherever I like." With that, she handed a $50 bill to Byte and stomped out of his room.

I turned to face Byte, utterly confused by everything that had happened in the last 10 minutes. He shrugged, "I was in the common room when she showed up with Ember. Ember went to talk to Phoenix, so I started talking to Keegan. We got to talking about robots, and before I knew it, we were building one, and you know the rest."

I glared at him. He held his hands up in surrender. "Look, brother, I'm not after your girl if that's what you're thinking. It's not often I meet someone with the same level of computer geekery as me, but I see her as a friend, nothing more," he explained.

I nodded my understanding. There was nothing I could say to make myself look like less of an asshole. "Anything new with her stepfather?" I grunted.

"Not a thing. His office has been radio silent," he said.

"Have you been able to dig up anything on Hastings or Hensley?" I asked.

Byte shook his head. "Sorry, brother. They're either clean or clever. I'm leaning toward clever. The only thing that seems the slightest bit off is neither of them has a lot of money coming in or available in liquid assets. Whatever they are doing with their money, I can't find it."

"Thanks for your help, brother," I mumbled.

CHAPTER SEVENTEEN

Keegan

That asshole! He didn't have to say it. I could see it written all over his face. He thought something was going on between me and Byte, something more than friendship. He couldn't be more wrong. Byte and I shared a love of computers, nothing more. Well, maybe a love for playing pranks, too.

I was fucking sick of Shaker and the way he was treating me. I tried, I really did, to give him the benefit of the doubt in regards to what happened between us in my kitchen. I knew he wouldn't hurt me, but I also knew those weren't the actions of the man I knew. The glazed-over, distant look in his eyes while he mercilessly fucked my mouth was a prime indicator that something was very, very wrong. And that would have been perfectly okay, if he would have talked to me about it instead of running away from me and avoiding me at all costs.

I stormed through the clubhouse all the way to my car without so much as a hello or goodbye to anyone. As soon as I got into my car, I realized it was still full of the supplies. Ember and I had been out picking up necessities for the horse farm when her father called and asked her to come by the clubhouse. None of the supplies were immediately needed or perishable, so I decided to go home and drop the supplies off at the barn the next day.

I pulled into my driveway and walked to my front door, not paying any attention to my surroundings. I stopped short when I finally noticed the man standing on my front porch. "What are you doing here?" I squeaked.

He moved toward me and extended his arm as if he was going to grab me when I was close enough. I stumbled backward in shock almost tripping over my own feet. I squealed when a hand landed on my shoulder, steadying me, and then my vision was filled with leather.

"Please refrain from touching Mrs. Marks,"

Kellan said, using his body to shield me from Lawrence.

"Excuse me? Who are you to stop me from hugging my stepdaughter?" Lawrence asked haughtily.

"I'm her bodyguard, sir. Per her husband's orders, no one is to put their hands on Mrs. Marks unless it is to directly prevent her from harm," Kellan replied without missing a beat.

Lawrence craned his neck around Kellan and asked, "Why does your husband feel the need for you to have a bodyguard? Are you in some sort of danger?"

His fake concern made me want to vomit all over his expensive shoes. I tried to mask my disgust and feigned indifference. "Not that I know of. His mother has a whole security team. I have one bodyguard. I didn't find that to be alarming. I guess it's a Marks thing. Now, back to my question, what are you doing here?"

"Would it be possible to speak with you without your guard dog between us?" Lawrence snidely asked.

"I'll be happy to step out of the way, if you don't mind having my gun trained on your forehead while you speak with her," Kellan said, not sounding the least bit concerned that he was openly threatening a senator.

Lawrence scoffed, "That won't be necessary. I had some business to tend to and was passing through the area. I thought I would stop by and visit with Keegan. I apologize if I frightened you, my child. I will be on my way."

Kellan escorted me to my front door where we watched Lawrence get into his car and drive away. "Thank you, Kellan. I have no doubt in my mind he had no intention of hugging me."

"Not a problem. If you could, next time, give me a heads up when you're leaving, I'd appreciate it. I was coming out of the restroom when you stormed out and almost missed you. Shaker would have had my ass, especially since Lawrence was here waiting for you," Kellan said.

I gasped, "I'm so sorry. It didn't even occur to me that someone would be tailing me. Here, put your number in my phone. I'll text you whenever I'm heading out if I don't see you." He handed my phone back to me as Shaker pulled into the driveway.

"Looks like my shift is over. I think I might try to catch up with Lawrence and see where he goes," Kellan grinned and leaped off my porch.

When Kellan reached his bike, he called out, "Keegan, don't forget to tell Shaker about

Lawrence showing up tonight." Then, he fired up his bike and disappeared into the night.

"The fuck he just say?" Shaker barked.

"When I got home tonight, Lawrence was waiting for me on the porch," I said and turned to go inside.

"What else?"

I sighed and decided to go ahead and tell him everything that happened so I could go to bed.

Shaker narrowed his eyes, "I bet that business he had to tend to had something to do with Preston."

"I hadn't thought of that, but, yeah, you're probably right." I didn't say as much, but it still didn't explain why he was at my house. He had never once dropped by to visit me since I moved out of his house years ago. But it was the move to grab me that had me unnerved. That and the fact that Lawrence was driving himself, something he never did. Was he going to try to force me to go somewhere with him?

Shaking my head to clear my thoughts, I continued on to my bedroom. "I'm going to bed. Night."

Shaker cleared his throat, "Keegan, I'm—"

"Don't. Just don't," I said and closed my bedroom door. I was too tired to deal with his shit. I barely managed to wash my face and brush my teeth before I flopped onto my bed and promptly fell asleep.

"Keegan," Shaker whispered, interrupting my thankfully dreamless slumber.

I dramatically crossed my arms over my eyes and groaned. "What?"

"I'm sorry."

"For what?"

"For waking you. For being an asshole at the clubhouse. For what happened in the kitchen, and the way I treated you after."

"Okay. Um, thank you. Goodnight," I mumbled and turned onto my side.

Shaker gripped my hip and rolled me back to him. "I didn't like finding you in Byte's room. Again. And when I heard the gunshots, my only concern was for your safety."

I sighed, "Thank you for protecting me. That, I appreciate. As for Byte, we are nothing more than fellow computer geeks who share a weird fondness for playing pranks."

"I do know that, and I'll try harder to respect your friendship with him."

"Good. Go to bed."

"Not yet. About the other thing. I, uh, I need you to under—"

"Shaker, you do not owe me any kind of explanation. I don't know what happened to you, and I don't need to know. If you want to talk about whatever it is, I'll be happy to listen, but don't share your secrets with me out of guilt."

He gently squeezed my hip with the hand he had yet to remove. "I'm not doing it out of guilt. I've needed to talk to someone about it for a long time, but I never felt like I could."

"And you do now?"

With his eyes locked on mine, he answered, "Yeah, I do. The look on your face after what I did." He closed his eyes and shook his head. "I don't ever want to see that look again. I want to explain, or at least try to."

"Whatever you tell me will not leave this room," I promised.

The corner of his mouth turned up in a small smile. "I know. It's one of the reasons I feel like I can talk to you about this."

He let go of my hip and settled against the headboard. "I started dating Beth during my senior year of high school. I joined the Marines right after graduation, and she was there waiting for me each time I came home. During my last deployment, she told me she had gotten pregnant when I was home during my leave. I made it home a couple of months before the birth. Long story short, I found out the baby wasn't mine in the delivery room."

When my brows furrowed in confusion, he cleared his throat and added, "Uh, racial features."

"Shaker, that's—"

"Let me get the rest out. If I don't do it now, I likely won't." At my nod, he continued, "I called Carbon, moved in with him, and joined the club. A year or so later, one of the club whores told me she was pregnant. Then, she told me she had an abortion a few days later. Turns out, she was lying about the abortion and the pregnancy. She was just trying to get money out of me."

I remained silent, unsure if there was more he wanted to share. He blew out a slow breath. "This is the part no one knows, and that's because I've never said it out loud."

Clearing his throat and clenching his fists, he blew me away with his next words. "After what those two bitches did to me, I promised myself I would never be in that position again. Because I wanted those babies, and it hurt like hell when they were taken from me. There's only one surefire way to prevent pregnancy, and that's abstinence of penetrative vaginal intercourse.

So, for the last five years, I haven't had sex with a woman in the traditional sense."

My brows furrowed in confusion. "That doesn't sound so bad, Shaker. Honestly, it's pretty fucking smart."

"Yeah, I thought it was, too, until I developed a problem of sorts because of it. Um, fuck, this is embarrassing. Okay, so, it got to where my body didn't respond to the typical things a heterosexual male's body should respond to. And when that bitch kidnapped me, she found out about my problem when she tried to rape me and couldn't."

"But Harper said you and Hilarie were fucking," I blurted. Of all the things I could have said, that was what came out of my mouth.

Shaker laughed sardonically. "We were. I just wasn't fucking her cunt."

Aaannnnd, that's when it clicked. Or part of it did. I couldn't help my reaction. I was shocked, and there was no way I could hide it. "You mean you only have anal sex with women?!"

"And oral, but I'm a taker not a giver," he added with a shrug.

"Okay, okay, um, that is a surprising revelation, but I'm obviously missing something. What's the problem?" So what if he liked anal sex. A lot of men did, or so I'd heard, and I was fairly certain all men enjoyed receiving oral sex.

He sighed in exasperation and turned away from me when he said, "I don't get hard for pussy like I used to. Or, I didn't, until you came along. And that pissed me off. So, the thing in the kitchen, yeah, I face fucked you like a whore because I was pissed at you. Or I thought I was. Guess I was really pissed off at myself and took it out on you."

Holy shit! I needed to say something, anything, but I was at a total loss for words. I got to my knees and wrapped my arms around his broad shoulders from behind. The man clearly needed a hug, and it was all I could think to do. And then I knew what to say. "Thank you for telling me. I wasn't upset with you for what happened, per se; I was upset about you leaving as soon as you, um, finished. I wasn't scared of you, but I knew something was wrong, and I wanted you to talk to me about it."

He reached up and curled his fingers around my clasped hands and gave them a gentle squeeze. "You're kind of awesome."

I honestly don't know what possessed me to say it, but before I could stop myself, I blurted, "Of course, I am. That's why I make your dick hard."

An animalistic sound came from his throat as he yanked me around to straddle his lap. "Yeah, you fucking do," he said and captured my lips in an all-consuming kiss. With one hand fisted tightly in my hair, he held me in place as he devoured my mouth.

"Shaker," I groaned against his lips.

He landed a sharp slap on my ass. "You call me Jacob when any part of me is inside of you," he growled.

I slid my hands into his hair and tugged, "Yes, Mr. Marks."

Another slap.

"Yes, sir."

Slap.

"Yes, Jacob," I breathed.

"Good girl. Now, let me apologize," he ordered.

"You don't have—"

"I fucking want to."

In one quick move, he tipped forward, so I fell back onto the bed while he yanked my sleep shorts and panties down my legs. I didn't have time to feel self-conscious or wonder if he liked what he uncovered because he was back on me before my clothes hit the floor.

I gasped when he buried his face between

my thighs. There was nothing tentative or unsure about his movements. The man was on a mission.

"Fuck, Keegan, your pussy tastes good," he groaned against my sex while he slipped one, then two fingers inside of me.

My fingers itched to thread through his hair and pull, but I didn't want to do anything to scare him off. The way he so effortlessly and efficiently tied my hands behind my back in the kitchen coupled with the history he just shared, I knew he had an issue with hands without him having to explicitly say it. So, I raised my hands above my head and grabbed onto the headboard.

My thoughts on hand placement were interrupted when Shaker lightly nipped at my clit with his teeth before he went back to licking and sucking. He slipped a third finger into my channel for a brief moment before I felt an extremely foreign yet not unpleasant sensation.

I tried to sit up so I could see what he was doing, but he let go of my clit with a pop and barked, "Don't move."

And I no longer cared what he was doing, because whatever it was felt fucking phenomenal. I could feel the tension building and knew I was going to come in a matter of seconds.

I felt him grin against the inside of my thigh as he removed his fingers while my body desperately tried to keep them inside. Panting and groaning, I sat up and scowled. "Why'd you stop?"

His grin grew even wider. The way his lips glistened from my arousal made him look downright sinful. He pinned me with his dark eyes. "Because you were about to come."

"Yes, isn't that—"

"Clothes off," he ordered.

"You first, big boy."

His grin went from sinful to feral. In a flash, he ripped his t-shirt over his head and pushed his pants to the floor. Apparently, Shaker wasn't a fan of underwear.

I was so wrapped up in staring at him in his full naked glory that I didn't realize he'd moved until he had the hem of my tank top fisted in his hands. Before I could utter a word, the sound of tearing fabric filled the room as the flimsy material parted to bare my chest to his hungry gaze.

He sucked in a breath and ran his teeth over his bottom lip. "Fuck, yes," he breathed, and then he was on me. My nipple was in his mouth, and his fingers were filling me once again.

"Oh, fuck, Jacob," I moaned. "I, I, I, shit. Want to touch you," I finally managed to say.

"Then fucking touch me," he said as he switched to my other breast.

At his words, my hands were everywhere. Tugging on his hair. Pressing against his chest. Clawing up his back. Squeezing his firm ass.

My mouth found his earlobe, and I nipped at it with my teeth. "Please. Fuck. Me."

His mouth never left my breasts, but one arm shot out to the side before he moved it between our bodies. His head came up, my nipple still deep inside his mouth, and his eyes found mine as he bucked his hips and filled me with his cock.

My eyes slammed shut, and my back arched from the bed. Holy. Shit. He was big. I'd seen him up close and personal, so I had a good idea of what to expect, or I thought I did.

When he didn't move, I opened my eyes to find him staring at me. Any other time, I would have appreciated his concern, but I was on the verge of something huge, and I was going to kill him if he didn't start fucking me properly in the next second. "Fucking move, Jacob," I panted, surely sounding like a crazed lunatic.

"Gladly," he growled and began ferociously

pumping his hips.

I clung to his shoulders and he moved above me, watching the muscles of his powerful arms flex as he thrust himself inside of me. My eyes followed my thoughts, and when the sight of our connection filled my vision, I was hit with an orgasm that damn well could have registered on the Richter scale.

The moment it subsided, I was hit with another, thankfully much smaller, orgasm. As my core started pulsing again, Shaker cursed and increased his pace. Half a dozen hard thrusts later, he buried his face in my neck and let out a groan that almost sounded pained.

"Fucking hell, woman," he breathed and softly kissed my sweat slicked neck.

***

What had we done? I knew exactly what we had done. Maybe, why had we done it was the thing to ask. No, the reason didn't matter. Our actions were what counted.

Damn it all to fucking hell.

Shit.

Piss.

Son of a motherfucking titty bitch!

"It's too early for the freak out you're having over there," Shaker rumbled from behind me.

Behind me in my bed.

My bed we spent all night fucking in.

"I'm sorry. I didn't know there was a designated freak out time!" I shrieked as I sat up and frantically glance around the room.

He sat up and grabbed my shoulders, "Calm down, Keegan. This is about last night, right?"

My eyes almost bugged out of my head. Was he serious? "Yes!!" I yelled.

He laughed, and I wanted to hit him. Hard. "We can still get the marriage annulled. We'll just have to lie and say we didn't consummate. Besides, what we did wasn't consummating a marriage. That was down and dirty fucking, and you know it," he grinned and moved to press his lips against my neck.

"You want me to lie to the court to get our fake marriage annulled?" I shrieked and shoved against his chest.

"Bring it down a few octaves, please. Yes, I want you to lie to the court. As long as there are no witnesses and you aren't pregnant with my baby, no one will know. Unless you would prefer to get divorced," he offered as he started pressing soft kisses under my jaw and down my neck.

Ugh. Were a handful of orgasms worth having a divorce on my record? Did it matter? He was right; it was too early to think about any of it, especially without coffee. I flopped back onto the bed and covered my eyes with my arm. "I'm going back to sleep," I mumbled.

"I don't think so," he said and rolled on top of me. There was no point in resisting. The deed had already been done, multiple times.

When I woke several hours later, I was alone and had been for some time as the sheets where Shaker had been were cold. It shouldn't have bothered me, but it did. I shouldn't have felt cheap and used, but I did. I shouldn't have shed any tears, but I did.

I let myself have a pity party for 15 minutes. Then, I got my ass out of bed and got dressed for the day. I needed to take the supplies Ember and I purchased the day before to the farm, and I thought a nice long ride would do me a world of good.

Kellan was in my driveway on his bike when I opened the front door. I let him know my plans for the day. I knew I would ride for hours, and I didn't want him to follow me around or wait on me. "I promise to call and wait for you before I leave the farm property. It would be just like the days I go to work, right?" I offered. Reluctantly, he agreed and left after helping me unload the supplies from my car.

Once I had everything put away, I saddled up my horse, Mystic, and let her run away with me. The property Ember and her father owned was huge. Most of the buildings were grouped together, leaving much of the land open and undeveloped. The open fields and wooded trails were perfect for pleasure riding.

As expected, Mystic ran full speed ahead to a pond tucked away behind a small copse of trees in the far corner of the property. I had ridden out there numerous times and never once ran into another person. It had become my secret place to escape, and my visit was way overdue. We trotted around the property and explored a new trail through one of the wooded areas before returning to the barn.

After I tended to Mystic, I led her back to her stall and gave her a few treats. Then, I opened the door and led my baby out. Blink was technically Mystic's baby, but I helped her deliver him and felt a special connection to both of them. At two years old, he was a beautiful thoroughbred colt. His coat was a warm grey with a slightly darker mane, and he had the most exquisite blue eyes. I spent some time working with him in the round pen. He was always difficult at the beginning of a training session, but by the end, he was typically much more compliant.

I turned to lead him back to the barn and nearly jumped out of my skin. Shaker was leaning against the railing of the pen watching me. When I startled, Blink did, too, and started to pull against the lead I was holding. He didn't fully rear up on his hind legs, but both front hooves left the ground several times. I didn't have to look to know Shaker would be climbing over the railing to help. "Stay back, Shaker! I can handle him," I said in a calm but firm tone. I remained calm and gently spoke to Blink, waiting for him to settle. Once he was calm again, I turned to Shaker and said, "Stay there while I put him in his stall."

I gave Blink some love and attention before leaving him with some treats. For the second time that day, Shaker's sudden appearance scared the crap out of me. He was leaning against the barn door, arms crossed, and staring at me. "Damn it, Shaker! You've got to stop doing that!" I scolded.

"Consider it payback," he muttered.

"Excuse me?"

"I didn't know where you were, and you weren't answering your phone. When I called Kellan, he told me you went to the farm and promised to call before you left. I've been looking for you for almost two hours. Then, when I finally found you, you were in the ring with a wild horse!" he said, progressively getting louder.

"He is not a wild horse; he's a baby, and I'm perfectly capable of handling him. And since when do I have to tell you where I'm going or what I'm doing?" I yelled, my balled fists going right to my hips.

"Since you agreed to let me protect you," he yelled back, pushing off the door and stalking toward me. "Since you became my wife!" He cupped my face with his hands and pressed his lips to mine, almost making me forget what an asshole he'd been.

Almost.

I pushed against his chest and took a step back. "Besides trying to slowly drive me insane, why are you here?" I asked.

He searched my eyes, for what I have no idea, before he answered with, "Are you upset with me about something?"

I huffed, "Answer my question first."

"You weren't answering your phone, and I needed to talk to you. Your turn," he grinned.

Oh, I could play that game, too. I returned his grin and raised it with a smirk, "Yes, I am." Question. Answered.

He threw his head back and laughed. I pushed against his chest again, trying to break his hold on me. Instead, he tightened his arms and pulled me closer. With his head nuzzled against my neck, he murmured, "I get it, wifey. Let me explain. I wasn't there when you woke up this morning because Byte called and asked me to come to the clubhouse. I started looking for you as soon as I finished with Byte."

He started gently kissing my neck, slowly working his way up. He placed his lips against the shell of my ear and breathed, "Still upset with me, wifey?"

His kisses felt so good. Being in his arms felt even better. But I wasn't going to let him distract me with his talented mouth. I pulled away from him and narrowed my eyes. "Are you still upset with me? If you don't have to tell me where you're going, I damn sure don't have to tell you where I'm going."

His eyes softened, "I didn't tell you where I was going because I didn't want to wake you. I also thought I would be back before you woke up. I'll leave a note next time."

Well, shit. I wasn't expecting him to have a valid excuse, or to offer a solution. "Okay. I guess I can send you a text and let you know where I am and what my plans are. Wait. You knew I was at the farm, so what was the problem?"

"The problem was that I couldn't find you. The farm is huge in case you haven't noticed. Where were you anyway?" he asked.

Did I dare tell him about my sacred little hideaway? I shrugged, "I was out riding Mystic. We started out riding through the open fields and ended up exploring a new trail through the wooded area. After that, I came back to the barn to work with Blink."

"Why didn't you answer your phone?"

"Honestly? When I have time to pleasure ride, I don't like to be interrupted. I never take my phone into the round pen when I'm working with a new horse. Even if I put it on vibrate, the sound of the vibration could startle the horse. It's too risky," I explained.

"I understand where you're coming from, on both points, but it's also too risky for you to be out riding without any means of calling for help. Same goes for working in the round pen.

I understand it's your job, but you're not alone when you're working. Today, you were alone," he said.

"So, now you're telling me what I can and can't do?"

"No, damn it. I don't want anything to happen to you!" he roared. He closed his mouth, and a look of shock washed over his face before he turned on his heels and walked away.

CHAPTER EIGHTEEN

Shaker

I had to walk away from her before I said something I didn't mean. When dealing with women, my go-to reaction was to lash out with hurtful words to mask my own feelings. I didn't want to do that with Keegan. When I couldn't find her or get her on the phone, I was scared. Finding her at the farm, carelessly putting herself in danger pissed me off. I climbed on my bike and took off. I needed to take a long ride to clear my head and calm down.

I was already on edge after talking to Byte. He called earlier that morning and asked me to come by the clubhouse. When I got there, he played a recording from the bug in Lawrence's office from the night before.

"*No. It did not go as planned, but there is no need for concern. I have a contingency plan, and we still have plenty of time before the deadline,*" Lawrence said.

"*Yes, you have mentioned that several times. However, it does not matter who is to blame; it will be both of our asses if our client does not receive his compensation on time.*"

"*He did what?*" Lawrence yelled. "*And you are just now telling me?*"

"*I swear, Harold, when this is over, you and I are going to revisit the terms of our business agreement,*" Lawrence growled.

"*Because I am the one doing all of the work while you are doing nothing other than reaping the benefits. I have no interest in that kind of partnership.*"

"*Then, I suggest you get off your lazy ass and help me fix this. Especially now that the amount has increased!*" Lawrence yelled followed by the sound of a phone slamming onto its base.

If we had made the calculations correctly, they had approximately one week left before they had to provide some kind of compensation to a male client. What kind of clients could Hensley and Hastings have? Obviously, they had some sort of business together, but we had yet to discover what it was. Until we had a name or location, we were at a standstill.

Regardless of how many times I went over the information we had, I couldn't piece it together. Nothing made sense. Hastings was involved in politics while Hensley was an investment banker. Both were involved in the horse industry, but each had their own farm. Something had happened leaving them responsible for compensating a client. Their original solution involved Preston, but he screwed it up. I presumed they meant Preston marrying Keegan, but how would that help them compensate a client?

The bottom line was we needed to find out what kind of business they were involved in and who their client was. From the sounds of it, they owed him money, but also some type of product. With only one week left, the danger to Keegan was at an all-time high. I just wish I knew what that danger was.

I rode for a few hours before returning to the clubhouse. The ride had calmed me, but I was no closer to figuring out what was going on. I entered the common room and was surprised at the number of brothers present. Usually, the place filled up much later in the evening.

After finding a seat at the bar, I got a beer from our newest prospect. It was shitty of me, but I couldn't remember the kid's name. I'd only taken two sips of my beer when my phone dinged. I wanted to ignore it, thinking it would be Keegan trying to continue our fight, but on the off chance it wasn't her or something was wrong, I needed to look.

Nope, not a message from Keegan. Instead, it was a video message from an unknown number. Chills ran down my spine as I tapped the message icon. When the message opened, I touched play and nearly choked at what was playing on my screen.

My mother was tied to a chair in her dining room. She had a gag in her mouth, and tears were streaming down her face. "Fuck!" I roared, getting to my feet.

The brothers in the common room fell silent at my outburst. Then, an electronic voice broke the silence, "Have $2.5 million ready for transfer in two hours, and your mother will remain unharmed."

I vaguely heard Coal's voice in the background as my vision blurred briefly before sharpening again. There was no room for emotions. I had to shut those off completely and focus on saving my mother.

"Phoenix is on his way," Coal called out to the room. "Emergency Church, now."

The following moments were a blur of activity. Phoenix came barreling into the clubhouse. I played the video for him, and he immediately started barking orders. He turned to me, "Do you have access to that kind of money?"

"Yes," I said and heard a few sharp inhales from the brothers in the room. "I could transfer it now if I knew where to send it."

"Good. Can you tell where they are in the video?"

"Yes, they are at my mother's house, in her dining room," I answered robotically. I'd managed to get control of my emotions and shut them down. I was in work mode and would stay that way until my mother was safe.

"Where is Keegan?" he asked.

"She's at the farm, working with her horses. Kellan is on her," I replied flatly.

Phoenix clapped his hands together loudly, "Byte, load whatever Shaker will need for the transfer in a cage. Edge, I want two cages following us. I need someone to stay behind with Harper and Annabelle. They're over at my house. Ember, Reese, and Keegan will be safe on the farm. The rest of you, we're rolling out in five."

"I'll stay with Harper and Annabelle," Badger volunteered.

"I'll ride with one of the boys taking a cage," Ranger announced. My head jerked in his direction, surprised by his declaration. Ranger hadn't ridden out on a mission like this with the club in several years. He claimed he was getting "too old for this shit." He shrugged, "I feel like I need to go. When I get a feeling about something, I don't ignore it."

I nodded, "Understood."

The brothers scattered to gather their things. Before I knew it, we were pulling out of the forecourt headed for my mother's house. It would take us longer than two hours to get there, but Byte had his equipment set up to make the transfer while we were on the road. He had my phone with him in the cage with Edge, so we didn't have to stop when the instructions for the transfer were sent to my phone.

About an hour and a half into the ride, the sound of a ringing phone filled my helmet. I had taken one of the club's extra phones and synced it to my helmet for the ride. As soon as I accepted the call, Byte started talking. "I've got the instructions. Your mother appears to be fine.

She is still bound and gagged, but I don't see any physical damage. I'm ready for your account information when you are."

I rattled off my login and password for the account that contained the majority of my assets immediately available for use. I braced myself for his reaction, and he did not disappoint. "Holy motherfucking shit, Shaker!"

"I know, but not now, okay?" I grumbled.

"Gotcha. All right, brother, it's ready to go when you say the word," he said.

"Did you set it up like we discussed?"

"Sure did. The money will show as pending in his account for one hour, which will give us plenty of time to get to your mother's house. If we find that she has been harmed, a few mouse clicks will void the transaction."

"Do you think we should tell him that?" I asked.

"Yeah, brother. I think it will ensure your mother's safety."

"Okay, do it," I said.

"Done. I'll let you know if I receive any more messages," Byte said and ended the call.

It took everything I had to focus on the road. My mind was working in overdrive. Was my mother okay? How did someone get past her security team? Why would someone target my mother?

Phoenix's voice filling my helmet broke me out of my thoughts. "Take the lead, Shaker." I glanced around and realized we were less than a mile from my mother's estate.

I broke formation and pulled in front, leading one of my worlds right toward the other. At least my mother already knew about the club. Hopefully, the club would be too focused on the situation at hand to worry about where I came from.

I led my brothers down the long, winding driveway that led to my mother's house. I came to a screeching halt and almost dropped my bike when I saw Keegan's car parked in the circle drive in front of my mother's house. "Fuck! Somebody find out where in the fuck Kellan is!" I roared as I burst through the front doors. I didn't concern myself with anything other than getting to my mother. I knew my brothers would cover me until each room was cleared.

I rounded the corner to find my mother still bound and gagged and thankfully, unharmed. Tears began pouring from her eyes when she caught sight of me. I pulled out my knife and quickly removed her gag while Phoenix was working on her hands and feet.

"Jacob," she shrieked as soon as I pulled the gag from her mouth. "You have to go get her! Don't waste time on me. I'm fine. Go! Now!"

"What are you talking about?" I asked, wondering if she truly was unharmed.

"Keegan! Lawrence took her! He told her he wouldn't harm me if she took my place. She arrived right after you transferred the money. He had everything timed perfectly. You have to find her. I don't know what he has planned, but it can't be anything good," she cried.

"Okay, okay. I can't leave you here alone. Where is your security team?" I asked.

"Not here. I'll tell you when there's more time," she said. "Now go find her!"

There was a commotion behind me. I turned to find Carbon and Duke struggling to hold back my mother's trusted bodyguard, Ronan. Ronan was snarling and cursing them for everything they were worth.

"Ronan!" my mother gasped.

"Let him through, brothers," I ordered. Carbon and Duke immediately released him.

He ran to my mother and cupped her face in his hands, "Jacquelyn, are you okay? When I discovered we had been deceived, I came as quickly as I could."

"I'm a bit shaken up, but otherwise, I'm unharmed," my mother said softly, tears staining her cheeks. Ronan wrapped her up in his arms and whispered soft words to her while she buried her face in his chest. Clearly, there was more to my mother's relationship with Ronan, but I would have to deal with that later.

"Mom, did Lawrence say where he was taking Keegan or why he needed her here?" I asked.

"No, nothing specific. He didn't say much while he was here. I think he thought he was keeping his identity hidden by wearing a mask and not talking, but one of the two men he had with him called him Senator, and Keegan called him Lawrence when she walked in," my mother said, shaking her head. "I'm sorry, son. That's all I can tell you."

"Thanks, Mom," I said and leaned in to place a kiss on her forehead. "I'm going to leave a few of my friends here with you and Ronan while we're out looking for Keegan."

"Okay. Please be careful and bring her back. I love you, Jacob," she said with tears in her eyes.

"I'll do my best. I love you, too," I said and turned to find my brothers so we could get a game plan together.

I found most of the club gathered in the kitchen, drinking coffee from my mother's antique fine china. I hoped Ronan kept my mother out of the kitchen until we were gone. She didn't place a lot of value on material things, but her china had sentimental value as well as monetary value.

"Mom confirmed it was Lawrence who held her for ransom. She didn't have anything to help us other than that. Has anyone gotten in touch with Kellan?"

As if on cue, Phoenix's phone rang. "Where the fuck are you, boy?" he growled into the phone. "Slow down. I can't understand you. Start again," Phoenix said as he placed his phone on speaker.

"I tried to call, but no one was picking up, and I couldn't keep calling while I was riding and tailing Keegan. She left the farm without telling me. I was waiting around outside the gates and followed when she tried to sneak off. She drove to some big ass house in Kentucky. She went inside the house and came out maybe two minutes later with Senator Hastings and two other men. Hastings grabbed her, shoved something into her neck, and she went limp. He put her in the car and drove to a barn in the middle of nowhere. I could see activity at the barn, but I couldn't tell what they were doing. I tried to call, but I couldn't get a signal out there. I'm about a mile down the road now. What do you want me to do, Prez?" Kellan spewed frantically.

"Text the location of the barn and go back to where you can keep an eye on the barn. We're at the big ass house now, and we're coming to you. If Hastings tries to leave before we get there, shoot him. I'll make sure nothing comes back on you," Phoenix said.

"Got it, Prez. I'm sending the location now. See you soon," Kellan replied and ended the call.

When the location came through, Prez and I led the way. According to the GPS, it would take around a half an hour for us to get there. Hastings better hope Keegan was unharmed when we arrived. He was already in for a world of hurt for what he had done to my mother and drugging Keegan.

The ringing filling my helmet startled me. When I answered, I was greeted with Byte's voice. "I've got some info on the location. It's listed as a residential property with a main residence and a small stable. A Mrs. Lois Hensley purchased the property, but a year later, Harold Hensley and

Lawrence Hastings were added to the deed. A few searches also show the property associated with a business named H & H Fillies."

"That makes no sense. They each have their own horse business. Why wouldn't they combine those two instead of starting a third one?" I wondered aloud.

"Don't know, brother. It seemed worth mentioning. I'll keep looking," Byte said.

Phoenix signaled for us to pull over when we were five minutes out. "We need to leave the bikes here and take the cages the rest of the way. The bikes will make too much noise, and we don't want them to know we're coming for our girl," Phoenix said.

Coal and Byte stayed with the bikes while the rest of us piled in the cages. We had been driving for more than five minutes when Phoenix's phone rang again. He answered it, laughed, and then instructed Edge to turn around. "We passed Kellan. Little fucker must be well hidden," Phoenix announced with a chuckle.

Kellan was waiting for us in the middle of the road. Edge and Dash pulled the cages to the side of the road and brothers started climbing out. Phoenix and Kellan were huddled close together talking. I couldn't handle waiting. I walked right up to them and butted in, "What's happening?"

Phoenix quirked a brow at my disrespect but didn't comment. "Kellan said a black sedan entered the property and stopped in front of the stables approximately 10 minutes ago. Hastings is there, not sure about Hensley. Give us a few minutes to survey the scene, and we'll get a plan together. They won't get past us, brother. We'll have your girl back soon," Phoenix said, clapping a hand on my shoulder.

Carbon, Phoenix, and Duke started scanning the property with binoculars. Ranger was holding a rifle and peering through the scope. "Phoenix," Ranger called, his voice eerily calm, "you need to see this."

Ranger handed his rifle to Phoenix. Phoenix peered through the scope, looked at Ranger, then put his eye back to the scope. "What the fuck?" he whispered.

CHAPTER NINETEEN

Keegan

I felt like shit. My head was pounding, my mouth felt like it was full of cotton, and my stomach was not a happy camper. What in the hell was going on? I groaned and tried to force my dry eyes open. I blinked a few times to get my eyes to focus and immediately wished I was still asleep.

I was sprawled on a nasty bed in a horse's stall. I got to my feet and scanned the space. There was nothing other than me, the bed, and a bottle of water in the stall. No way in hell was I drinking that. I had to remain calm. Panicking wouldn't do anything to help me. I needed to think. Where was I and how did I get there?

It all came back to me at once. Jacquelyn tied to a chair. Lawrence offering to release her in exchange for me. Leaving the farm without telling anyone. Leaving Jacquelyn's house with Lawrence. Lawrence grabbing me followed by a sharp stinging sensation in my neck. That bastard had drugged me. Why would he do that?

It didn't matter why he did it. I needed to find a way to get out of the stall and far away from him before he came back. I already knew it wouldn't be there, but I had to check. Almost hesitantly, I reached for the back pocket of my jeans to feel for my phone, which wasn't there. Shit. I scanned the room again looking for anything I could use to defend myself or help me escape.

The sound of voices had me freezing on the spot. My heart felt like it was going to beat right out of my chest. I needed more time to come up with a plan. I did the only thing I could think of to buy myself more time. I quietly crept to the bed and arranged myself in the position I was in when I had woken. Closing my eyes, I tried to breathe as evenly as possible and willed my heart to slow down.

The door to the stall slid open, and footsteps approached. "How much did you give her?

Shouldn't she be awake by now?" Mr. Hensley snidely asked.

"I administered the correct dosage, Harold. Some take longer to rouse. I assure you, this is better than her screaming and disturbing the others. We'll check back in a bit. When is Rowe due to arrive?" Lawrence asked.

Rowe? Others?

"Within the hour. He won't be happy if she is still knocked out from the drugs when he arrives," Harold said.

"If she has not woken by the time he arrives, I will give her the medication to reverse the effects of the sedative. Relax, Hensley. In less than an hour, we will give him the money and the girl. Then, we can finally put this behind us," Lawrence said casually.

It took every ounce of control I possessed to force myself not to react to his words. I knew I had to keep still or I would blow my only shot at getting away before this Rowe person arrived. Once the stall door closed and I heard a lock slide into place, I remained still for several beats before resuming my search of the stall. Eyeing the bed, I briefly wondered if I could use part of the frame as a weapon.

The stall door suddenly opened to reveal

Lawrence sneering at me. "I knew you were faking, you stupid little cunt. Here's what's going to happen. My business associate will arrive soon. You are going to leave with him without causing any problems. If you do that, I will guarantee no harm will come to Jacquelyn, Gabriella, or your beloved husband. If you resist, I will kill them all."

I gasped, and the tears fell freely from my eyes. "You would kill your own daughter?"

He shrugged, "It would not be my first choice, but I could make it work for me. Losing a wife and my only daughter in the span of five years would surely win me thousands of sympathy votes."

He was a monster. A monster I was going to destroy as soon as I had the opportunity. Until then, I would have to go along with his plan and pray that I wasn't too broken by the end of it. "I will do whatever I have to to make sure Gabriella is kept safe," I said vehemently.

Lawrence smiled cruelly, "That's what I thought." He turned and left me alone in the stall to wait for my next hell to begin.

I couldn't stop the tears or the overwhelming anger surging through me. My mother was a great mother. Until Lawrence came along, her life revolved around me, and she seemed content with that. I recall hearing her say numerous times, "Being a parent is the most important job one can have." So how did my dedicated, loving mother subject not one, but two children to a man like Lawrence? I let my anger fuel me and give me strength. I would need it to survive whatever lay ahead.

I was pacing the stall and trying to keep myself amped up when the stall door slid open. A man I had never seen before stepped inside and closed the door. My feet were rooted to the spot while I studied him carefully. He was not at all what I expected. He was dressed in a tailored three-piece suit and carried himself with an air of authority. In another situation, I would have described him as handsome.

He took a step forward, and I immediately took a step back. He kept his eyes trained on me but did not try to move closer. He raised one finger to his lips in the universal sign to be quiet. Then, ever so slowly, he pulled his suit jacket to the side to reveal a gold badge attached to his belt. It couldn't be. My eyes widened and shot to his. He nodded once and mouthed, "Play along."

I glanced at the badge again. I had never seen an FBI badge before, but the one he had looked authentic. Still, I didn't know if I should trust him or not. He didn't give me time to think it over. He stepped close and whispered one sentence that had me sagging with relief, "I'm friends with Phoenix Black."

A loud sob escaped from me. I was safe or would be soon. And Lawrence was about to have his ass handed to him by the FBI. I straightened my spine and gave a curt nod to the agent. I would play along and help him take down Lawrence.

The agent leaned closer and whispered, "I need you to fight me or put up a struggle."

"He told me he would hurt my sister if I didn't go with you quietly," I whispered back.

The agent's jaw clenched. "I'm going to carry you out over my shoulder. Try to make it sound like you are quietly crying. Ready?"

I nodded. I was more than ready. Even though I was thrilled about the unexpected turn of events, I was still upset enough by the entire ordeal to produce plenty of genuine tears. The agent bent his knees, hoisted me over his shoulder, and carried me out of the stall. I shuddered and sobbed as he strode toward the exit.

"Once the wire transfer has been verified, I will be on my way," the agent said.

"I can assure you the money has been transferred to your account, Mr. Rowe," Lawrence promised.

The agent scoffed, "Assure away, but I will verify it with my own eyes. You've given me no reason to trust you."

"Very well," Lawrence replied tightly. "Do you require any assistance with your filly?"

"None whatsoever. Unlike you and your partner, I'm quite capable of handling a female without issue," the agent spat and slapped me on the ass. I clutched his shirt and whimpered as my cries turned into sobs.

I kept my eyes squeezed shut. I didn't want to see Lawrence ever again, unless he was in handcuffs or behind bars. I felt the agent moving, and then I was turned right side up and placed in a car. The agent slid into the back beside me and pulled out a tablet. He tapped on the screen a few times and then told the driver we were ready to leave.

Turning to face me, he extended his hand, "Hi, Keegan. My name is Luke Johnson. I'm a special agent with the FBI. I've been working undercover to bring down Hastings and Hensley. I'm going to take you to a safe house right now. You'll need to stay there until the investigation is complete."

"What? How long will that take?" I shrieked.

"I don't know exactly, but it shouldn't be long. I'm sorry, but if Lawrence were to catch sight of you roaming around freely, it could blow the entire case," he said softly.

"I need to call my husband and let him know I'm okay. He's probably on his way to kill Lawrence as we speak."

"I can't let you do that. We can't risk your location being discovered, and we need your husband's reactions to be genuine," he said.

"I'm telling you right now, Agent Johnson, if my husband gets his hands on Lawrence, you won't have a case because He. Will. Kill. Him."

Luke's eyebrows shot up. "You really think a member of the Marks family would commit murder?" he asked skeptically.

"Do you really think a member of Blackwings MC wouldn't?" I shot back.

His brows furrowed in confusion. "Aren't you married to Jacob Marks?"

"Yes, I am. Jacob is also known as Shaker, Blackwings MC Road Captain, Original Chapter," I said proudly.

Luke shook his head. "No, Shaker's name is Jay Markus."

"That's a fake name he uses to keep people from finding out about his money," I countered.

Before Luke could reply, the driver said, "Luke, we have a problem."

"Fuck! What is it?" Luke barked.

"Armed men on motorcycles are blocking the road," he said as he glanced in the rearview mirror, "in both directions."

I folded my arms across my chest and smirked, "Told ya."

"Fuck!" he cursed. "Stop the car. Keegan, get your head down and do not get out of the car. Thomas, call Peterman and let him know what's going on. See if we can get this shit expedited."

Luke stepped out of the car with his hands in the air. I assumed he would close the door and go talk to Phoenix, but that's not what happened. He used the car door as a shield and spoke to the club from a distance. "She's in the car, and she's fine. Please lower your weapons," Luke said calmly.

"What in the hell is going on, Luke?" Phoenix growled.

"An undercover investigation that you and your club are about to blow wide open. I'll explain, but right now we need to get out of here," Luke said. "You and Shaker can follow the car, but the rest need to scatter."

"I'm not moving until I see for myself that Keegan is okay," Shaker barked.

I heard Luke sigh heavily, "Fine. Keegan, come on out."

I stepped out of the car and scanned the crowd of men for Shaker. When my eyes landed on him, I saw his body visibly relax. "I'm okay, Shaker. I promise." Suddenly, I remembered Jacquelyn. "Is your mother okay?"

"Yeah, baby, she's good," he said.

"Save the chit-chat for later, kids. We need to move out, now," Luke ordered and motioned for me to get back into the car.

As soon as the door closed, we were moving again. "What did Peterman say?" Luke asked anxiously.

"After a string of expletives, he said to bring the girl to the safe house as planned and the rest of the team will meet us there. Once she is secure, we will go pick up Hastings and Hensley. You need to get her statement now," the driver, Thomas, said.

I spent the remainder of the drive recounting the events of the day, as well as the pertinent events over the past few months. Luke took down everything I said with little to no reaction.

It was as if nothing I said shocked him. I found it unsettling. "...and the weirdest thing was when I showed up at his house unannounced and found him giving it to Hensley from behind."

Luke choked and coughed, his eyes widened in surprise, "Excuse me?"

I laughed, "So, you are capable of being shocked? Just checking."

He gave me a small smile, "Sorry. It's easier to handle investigations such as these when you remain detached. Plus, most of what you told me I already knew or expected."

"I see. So, can you tell me why the FBI is investigating Lawrence? Obviously, he kidnapped me and handed me over to someone against my will, but that didn't happen until today. What had he been doing to garner the attention of the FBI?" I asked curiously.

"I can share some details, but you have to keep them to yourself until I say otherwise. I'm serious about that. If you don't, you could find yourself being charged with obstruction of justice or interfering with a federal investigation," he said.

"Understood," I replied. The story would spread like wildfire once the media got a hold of it. That meant reporters would be all over me.

Not. Fun.

"Lawrence Hastings and Harold Hensley are being investigated for their involvement in profiting from and running a prostitution ring, as well as money laundering, racketeering, and human trafficking."

"Say what now?" I blurted.

"I can't tell you much more than that right now. Until we have them both in custody with formal charges, the case is considered open, which means I can't openly discuss it," he said.

"My sister," I gasped. "What will happen to her once Lawrence is in custody?"

"If he doesn't have provisions in place, he will need to make some quickly, or the courts will decide what to do with her," Luke explained.

"I will cooperate with you and help in any way I can, but I want full custody of Gabriella. Do you think you can help me make that happen?" I asked.

Luke smiled, "Yes, I think that's doable."

When we arrived at the safe house, Phoenix and Shaker were beside the rear passenger door before Thomas could shut off the engine. I opened the door and was immediately engulfed by Shaker. He slid one hand around my back while the other gently cupped the back of my head. Pressing me against his chest, he buried his face in my neck. "Keegan," he breathed.

I wrapped my arms around his neck and relished in the feel of his body against mine, his comforting scent surrounding me. My fingers threaded through his hair, "Jacob, you came for me."

He pulled back and met my eyes, "Of course, I did. You're my wife." Then, his mouth was covering mine in a scorching kiss. I moaned into his mouth and tried in vain to pull him closer. His hands were everywhere, as if he was checking to make sure I was really there.

"You might need to get the water hose to separate them," Phoenix chuckled.

Shaker broke the kiss but didn't release me. I buried my face in his cut, slightly embarrassed by our indecent display of affection in front of Phoenix and Luke.

Luke cleared his throat, "Let's go inside."

We followed Luke into a nondescript townhouse. Not exactly what I pictured when I thought of a safe house, but I supposed that was the point. Once we were settled in the living room, Luke introduced us to the agents who would be staying with me while another team of agents went after Lawrence and Mr. Hensley.

When my eyes landed on the female agent, I instantly recognized her and couldn't contain my disbelief. "You're an agent?"

Before she could answer, Shaker stepped in front me of. "What's wrong?"

"Nothing. She was Lawrence's date for the charity ball," I said and stepped around his big body. "You're good. I seriously thought you were a complete idiot."

She stifled a laugh and nodded. "Just doing my job. It's nice to officially meet you. I'm Agent Lindstrom," she said kindly and extended her hand to me.

Another man stepped forward to shake my hand, "And I'm Agent Hall. We'll be staying here with you until Agent Johnson gives the all clear." He directed his attention to Phoenix and Shaker, "Are you two staying or going?"

"Staying," the both answered at the same time. I had no doubt Shaker would all but refuse to leave my side, but I assumed Phoenix would want to get back to Annabelle.

"Okay. There are agents in the townhouses on either side of this one as well. All incoming and outgoing signals are blocked, so there'll be no phone calls, texts, emails, or contact of any kind with anyone until you've heard from me,"

Luke explained.

"How will we hear from you?" I asked. The geek in me had to know.

Luke flashed me a grin, complete with dimples, "We have our ways, Mrs. Marks." With that, Luke walked out the door.

The silence that followed his departure was uncomfortable, to say the least. I felt like I was being examined under two different microscopes. The agents were watching and analyzing my every move. Phoenix and Shaker seemed to be fixated on my face, as if waiting for me to have a breakdown. It was too much.

"Stop staring at me! I'm not going to try to escape or break one of the communication rules, and I'm not going to have an emotional meltdown," I yelled.

Agent Hall nodded, "We'll be in the kitchen." Agent Lindstrom nodded once as well and followed Agent Hall.

Phoenix and Shaker were both grinning at me. "What?" I huffed in exasperation.

Shaker chuckled lightly, "I wasn't sure if you were truly okay or not until you put everyone in their place."

"I appreciate your concern, but I'm fine. I'm just ready for this to be over," I said.

CHAPTER TWENTY

Shaker

We waited for hours before we heard anything from Luke. The tension in the room grew as the minutes turned into hours. The agents assured us that these things took time and we were nowhere near the time to start worrying. Easy for him to say. His immediate future wasn't relying on the outcome of the next few hours.

Phoenix was asleep on the sofa, and I was lost in my thoughts with Keegan snuggled into my side when we heard a phone ringing in the kitchen. My ears strained to make out the words spoken. Moments later, Agent Hall entered the living room, his expression giving nothing away.

"Hastings and Hensley are in police custody. You three are free to go, but I would strongly advise you to keep the events of this evening to yourselves for the time being. Luke will be in touch."

I turned to Keegan to find her smiling from ear to ear. "Let's go home," she said.

"We have to stop by my mother's house first. She won't be satisfied until she has seen you with her own eyes. Plus, the rest of the brothers are there waiting for us," I told her.

"You're kidding, right?" she asked.

"No, why?"

She laughed. "I just can't picture a bunch of bikers lounging around on the antique furniture in your mother's sitting room. Maybe they're sipping tea from her fine china, too."

"They were slurping coffee from it when I left," I deadpanned.

Her eyes widened, "We should probably get moving."

The ride back to my mother's house seemed to pass by much faster. We pulled into the circular drive and were met with a sea of biker's standing on the front steps, my mother up front and center. She rushed forward and pulled Keegan and me in for a hug the moment our feet were on the ground. "Oh, thank goodness! I've been so worried. Are you both okay? What happened? Where's Lawrence?"

"Mom, slow down. We're fine. Let's go inside, and we'll fill everyone in on what happened," I said calmly.

"Of course, dear. Lead the way," she said and made a show of gesturing toward the front doors.

Once inside, everyone gathered in the family room to hear the story. "We can't go into much detail, and I'll explain why in a moment," I began. "Keegan's stepfather and his business partner were unknowingly being investigated by the FBI for running a whore house as well as selling women. Lawrence used my mother to get a ransom from me and to lure Keegan here so he could take her with the intent to sell her. Actually, he did sell her; he just didn't know the man he sold her to was actually Agent Luke Johnson." Gasps and murmurs sounded throughout the room, but I continued with the story. "Luke was able to extricate Keegan and get her to a safe house without incident, which is where we have been for the last several hours. We were allowed to leave when we received word that Senator Lawrence Hastings and Harold Hensley were in police custody." Hoots and hollers erupted from everyone, including my refined mother.

"There are still some loose ends to tie up, so keep this to yourselves for the time being. We don't want anything to possibly jeopardize the case," Phoenix ordered. The brothers murmured their agreement.

My mother loudly clapped her hands to garner the room's attention. "Who's hungry?" I couldn't help but laugh. My mother was without fail a wonderful hostess, regardless of the circumstance.

By the time we finished dinner, it was getting late. We needed to get on the road to get back to Croftridge if we were going. I wasn't sure if Keegan was up for the ride or not. "Do you want to go home tonight or in the morning?" I asked quietly.

"Tonight, please. I need a shower, and I want to put on my own pajamas and sleep in my own bed," she said with a yawn.

That yawn was enough to tell me she wouldn't last on the back of my bike. We said goodbye to my mother and promised to call the moment we arrived home safely. I tossed my keys to Byte and climbed into a cage with Keegan and Edge.

"What are you doing?" she asked.

"You're tired, and you were drugged earlier today. It's safer for you to ride back in the cage, and I want to ride with you, so I'm letting Byte ride my bike back," I explained.

She smirked, "Is that considered a romantic gesture for a biker?"

I shrugged, "I wouldn't call it romantic, but it's a big deal to let someone else take your bike."

"Oh, well, thank you, kind sir," she said sweetly, exaggeratingly blinking her eyes.

"You know, it's not the first time I've let a brother take my bike to stay with you."

"It isn't?" she asked and rested her head on my shoulder.

"Guess you don't remember. When I found you on the side of the road, you asked me to stay with you."

"And you did?"

I kissed the top of her head, "Yeah, baby, I did."

I was right. She was asleep within 10 minutes of being on the road. "So, what happens now?" Edge asked.

"I'm not sure. I guess we wait for the story to hit the media outlets. The press is going to be all over the two of us. I need to make sure a brother or a prospect shadows her when I'm not with her until this passes," I said, more to myself than to Edge.

"Did you officially call off Kellan?" Edge asked. I shook my head. "Problem solved. He'll keep shadowing her until you say otherwise."

"We need to patch him in. He has more than earned his cut as far as I'm concerned," I said. Kellan's quick thinking and intuition had saved Keegan several times. I would forever be grateful to him for keeping Keegan out of harm's way.

"So, are we going to talk about you being filthy rich and no one knowing about it?" Edge asked jovially.

"Nope," I replied and crossed my arms over my chest, effectively ending the conversation.

***

I woke to the sound of my phone ringing. Judging by the minuscule amount of light streaming in from the windows, it was too early for anyone to be calling with good news, which was confirmed the next second when I saw Phoenix's name flashing on the screen.

"Morning, Prez," I grumbled into the phone.

"Luke called just now. The media has gotten wind of a scandal involving Senator Hastings and prominent businessman Harold Hensley. They are holding a press conference later today. I know you were expecting some attention from reporters, but it sounds like it's going to happen sooner than you thought," Phoenix said.

Fuck! I was hoping Keegan would at least have a day to recuperate before the press started hounding her. "Thanks for letting me know, Prez."

"Think about staying at the club for a few days. Or Ember could set you up in a room on the farm. Just until the vultures get bored and leave town," he suggested.

"Thanks, Phoenix. I'll talk to Keegan about it," I said and disconnected the call.

"Talk to me about what?" she asked, her voice still raspy from sleep.

I rolled to my side to face her and cupped her cheek with my hand. "Staying at the clubhouse or the farm until the media storm passes. Parts of the story have already leaked, and Luke just let Phoenix know they will be holding a press conference later today," I explained.

"The farm. Since I work there, I wouldn't have to leave the property," she said.

"Okay," I said softly. "I'll call Ember and make the arrangements. We should probably get over there sooner rather than later."

"Sounds good. I'll get up and get my things together. How long do you think I'll need to stay at the farm?" she asked.

"I wouldn't think any longer than a week," I guessed.

While Keegan packed, I called Ember to reserve a room. To my surprise, she offered us a fully furnished cottage to use as long as we needed. I readily accepted, happy to have the extra privacy.

We were packed and headed to the farm within the hour. Thankfully, we didn't run into any reporters between Keegan's house and the farm. I fully expected to see a few standing outside of the gates at the farm property.

Keegan was pleasantly surprised when I pulled up to the house Ember provided for us. I have to admit; I was impressed with the place. It was a cottage in every sense of the word—small, quaint, charming. I thought it was perfect. Keegan, however, had a different opinion.

"Were you planning on staying here, too?" she asked.

"Yes," I answered slowly, unsure of why she would even ask.

"Where are you going to sleep? There's only

one bedroom, and I don't believe this is a pull-out sofa," she said.

I should have known this was coming, but it honestly hadn't crossed my mind until she mentioned the sleeping arrangements. Now that Lawrence was in custody and she was no longer in danger, we could end our marriage and go our separate ways. But there was no way I was letting that happen without a fight.

I stalked toward her, feeling much like a dangerous predator. When I reached her, I dipped down and hoisted her over my shoulder, carrying her to the bedroom. I tossed her onto the bed and came down on top of her, my hands braced on either side of her head. "I'm sleeping with you, wifey," I said and immediately covered her mouth with mine, not giving her even a second to protest.

She still tried though. She weakly pushed at my chest and tried to buck me off with her hips as she mumbled something against my lips. When I didn't remove my mouth from hers, she gave in and melted into the kiss. Once she surrendered, it didn't waste any time showing her what I was unable to put into words.

She watched intently as I carefully removed her clothes followed by my own. Then, I took my time and worshipped her body, kissing and touching every square inch. When she tugged on my hair and whispered my name, I opened the condom I'd grabbed from my jeans and slicked it over my shaft.

Moving over her, I cupped her cheeks in my hands and softly kissed her while I slowly sank inside of her. She let out a contented sigh when I was fully seated. I pressed my forehead to hers and held her gaze as I started to move with slow and even thrusts.

I felt her body tense and knew she was close. Capturing her lips, I maintained my pace as she clung to my shoulders and tightened her legs around my hips. When I felt her internal walls start to flutter, I let myself go, and we climaxed together.

I stayed where I was, enjoying the connection with shared, for as long as I could. Then, I got up and quickly dealt with the condom before climbing back into bed with her and pulling her sated body flush against mine. Moments later, we both drifted off to sleep.

I woke before she did, and while I wanted to stay in bed with her and keep her in my arms, I couldn't. So, reluctantly, I got up and got in the shower. Despite trying to be quiet, Keegan woke while I was getting dressed.

"Jacob," she said softly, "we have to talk about this."

"Talk about what?" I asked, as if I didn't know what she meant.

"This," she gestured between the two of us. "Us. The marriage. Just, all of it."

"I think we should hold off on that discussion for now," I said. I was an asshole for doing it, but I played the only card I had left. "I don't think we should do anything in regards to the marriage until you're granted custody of your sister."

Her eyes widened at my words, and then she was nodding her head, "I hadn't thought about that, but I completely agree. Trying to get custody of my sister while simultaneously divorcing a man I've been married to for less than a month probably wouldn't be the best idea."

I leaned forward and placed a soft kiss on her lips. "I need to go to the clubhouse. Do not leave the farm property for any reason whatsoever. Okay?"

"I have no intention of leaving the farm. I'll probably be at the new barn all day trying to get caught up. I'm almost afraid to find out how far behind schedule I am," she said.

"Oh, I forgot to tell you. When I talked to

Ember about staying on the property for a few days, she said to tell you to take as much time off as you needed. According to her, you were ahead of schedule and Duke has pitched in so you wouldn't fall behind," I said.

"Really?" she squealed. "They are too good to me! Now, I'll be able to spend some time with my babies."

"Make sure you have your phone on you or at least have it nearby, especially if no one else is around."

"Yes, sir," she said with a wink, making my dick twitch.

Damn her.

***

When I left for the clubhouse, I was surprised to find no reporters hovering outside the gates of the farm. I found out why 20 minutes later. They were all hovering across the street from the clubhouse. The prospect on gate duty was quick to let me in and close the gates before any of them could make it across the road.

I shook my head. Now that I had been spotted entering the clubhouse, they would wait for me to leave and follow me back to the farm. I was assuming the lack of media presence meant they hadn't discovered the farm's association with the club yet. Maybe I could get by them unnoticed in a cage.

I entered Church and took my seat, noting that we were still waiting on a few brothers to arrive. When I saw Luke Johnson sitting in a chair off to the side, I was instantly on alert. His presence in the clubhouse wasn't a good sign.

"What's he doing here?" I asked Phoenix, jerking my chin in Luke's direction.

"He has some information to share with the club. I wanted to wait for all of the officers, but if they're not here in the next five minutes, we'll get started without them," Phoenix grumbled. It didn't sound like he was happy to see Luke either.

True to his word, Phoenix closed the door at the five-minute mark and called the meeting to order. Everyone except Badger was there. "Luke has some information to share with us. Keep your mouths shut and let him talk," Phoenix ordered.

Luke stepped up to the table and began, "We will be holding a press conference today regarding the arrests of Senator Lawrence Hastings and Harold Hensley. Obviously, the media is already aware of Jacob's and Keegan's affiliation with the Blackwings MC. I would advise you to ignore them as best you can. Don't say anything other than 'no comment' to them. The reason I'm here has to do with why we began investigating Hastings and Hensley."

He shifted his weight and cleared his throat. "When we raided the farm property a year and a half ago, we discovered ties between Octavius Jones and Hastings. Octavius was helping Hastings and Hensley get into the human trafficking business," he said. He grimaced and turned to face Phoenix.

Phoenix gripped the edge of the table so hard the wood creaked. He growled low in his throat and barked, "Say it."

Luke stood and squared his shoulders. "Hastings was the man who was going to purchase Ember."

Chaos erupted in the room. Men were shouting and cursing. Phoenix was vibrating with rage while Carbon struggled to restrain him. Duke was also struggling to contain a furious Dash. And I was on my feet moving to stand in front of Luke. The door burst open to reveal Ranger with his rifle at the ready. "What in the fuck is going on in here?" he bellowed.

Everyone froze, and no one said a word. "Well? One of you fuckheads start talking."

Luke, the only non-member in the room, answered, "I just gave them some shocking and rather disturbing news."

"And that was?" Ranger snapped.

"Senator Hastings was the man who tried to buy Ember from Octavius. That was ultimately what spawned the investigation into Hastings and Hensley," Luke explained.

"And?" Ranger asked.

"That's it," Luke replied.

"So, why in the hell is everyone so pissed off?" Ranger asked incredulously.

Phoenix growled, "He should've told me who tried to buy my baby girl when he found out!"

"Why? So you could go down for murdering a government official? Pipe down and let the man explain," Ranger ordered.

Phoenix heaved in a deep breath, and I watched in awe as he reined in his rage. He remained silent but gave Luke a sharp nod.

"I couldn't tell you when we first discovered the connection because we weren't sure what they were involved in. By the time we discovered it was women, a full-blown federal investigation had been launched. Ember was safe, Octavius was dead, and his men had been arrested. I didn't have a justifiable reason to tell you," Luke explained.

"Why wasn't Hastings arrested before now?" Dash demanded from the spot where Duke had him pressed against the wall.

Luke shook his head, his eyes cast to the table, "Believe me, if I could have arrested him, I would have. We didn't have enough proof. We needed solid evidence before we could accuse a senator of human trafficking. Since the transaction regarding Ember wasn't completed, we had to wait for another one. It took him a long time to find another supplier, for lack of a better word, after Octavius died. When we got word that he had found someone, I went undercover as a potential buyer. We had everything set up over a month ago, but the girl vanished. The money had already been transferred, but we needed the girl for the charges to stick. None of us wanted to wait another year, so I put some pressure on him for losing the girl I had purchased. I demanded half of my money back and a new girl, which is where Keegan came into the picture."

"Is that why Lawrence was trying to force Keegan to marry Preston Hensley?" I asked.

"No, that was for the money," Luke replied.

"What money?"

"Keegan has a trust fund that's only accessible once she is married or turns 25 years old, whichever comes first. Hastings and Hensley wanted her to marry Preston to gain access to the trust so they could pay me off," Luke explained.

I cocked my head to the side. "That doesn't make sense. She already has access to her trust fund."

Luke nodded in agreement. "Yes, she does have access to one, but she has two, which she should have access to since she married you. You didn't know?"

I shook my head slowly, "No, I didn't, and I don't think she does either."

CHAPTER TWENTY-ONE

Keegan

I was pleasantly surprised when I arrived at the barn. Duke must have been busting his ass to make sure we didn't fall behind. I owed him big time. I spent a few hours taking care of things for the barn. When I was finished, I started working with Blink. As much as I didn't want to, I kept my promise and put my phone on one of the fence posts.

It had been a few days since I had been able to work with Blink and it showed. Once I got him warmed up, he started cooperating with me, which was a good thing because we needed to run some time trials. I left Blink in the round pen and went back to the office to turn the cameras on and make sure the computer was ready to go. We had a brand new, state of the art race timing system, and I was itching to try it out.

As I was turning to leave the office, something on the desk caught my eye. I smiled as I picked up the set of Bluetooth earbuds with a sticky note attached to the front.

Sync these with your phone and stay safe out there.

Shaker

I smiled at his thoughtfulness. It was a great idea, and I was a little disappointed that I hadn't thought of it myself.

I synced the earbuds and made sure they were securely attached before I led Blink to the track. I was slightly nervous. He had only been on one other track before, and I wasn't sure how he would do in a new setting. There was only one way to find out. So, I pulled on my big girl britches and climbed in the saddle.

Blink's excitement seemed to match my level of anxiety. He was chomping at the bit, pun intended. I held him at the starting line for several seconds before shouting, "Go!" He took off without much encouragement from me, and I cherished every second of it. There was nothing but the wind, the track, Blink, and me. We rounded the last curve, and I just knew this was going to be one of his best times yet. When we crossed the finish line, I threw my hand in the air, fist-pumping and cheering like we had won a monumental race.

I was dying to check out the video and see the official time, but I knew a proper cool-down was imperative for Blink. I took care of Blink and made a beeline for the office only to faceplant into a wall of muscle.

"Whoa! Where's the fire?" Duke asked.

"Sorry. I wasn't expecting anyone else to be here," I mumbled.

He chuckled, "Neither was I."

"Thank you for taking care of things around here for me. I really appreciate it," I said sincerely.

He waved his hand dismissively, "Don't mention it. It was the least I could do after the way I treated you. Besides, there wasn't much to do anyway."

"Do you need any help over at your barn?" I offered.

He shook his head. "No. I guess Ember hasn't had a chance to tell you yet. She hired a new stable hand for us to share. Since you only have two horses here, I was able to pitch in at your barn while he took care of the horses at my barn," he explained. "Now, where were you headed in such a hurry?"

I grinned, "Follow me, and I'll show you." Duke followed me to the office and took a seat. I turned the computer screen so we could both see and hit play. We watched in silence as Blink and I casually made our way to the starting line. When I yelled and Blink bolted from the line, I stared at the timer in astonishment. Blink was faster than I thought. Much faster.

Duke whistled low and long, but he waited until we crossed the finish line to comment. "That fucker is fast. Is he yours?"

I beamed proudly, "Yes. He's Mystic's colt. I helped her deliver him."

"Are you going to race him?" he asked.

"I'm not sure," I said, still dazed by the time flashing at the bottom of my screen. "I had no idea he was that fast. You think it was a fluke?"

"No, I don't. Next time you run him, let me know, and I'll manually clock you," he offered.

"Thanks," I replied dumbly. I daydreamed about racing horses when I was a little girl, but I never thought it would be a possibility. I wanted to be excited about the prospects, but I was afraid to get my hopes up. Based on my previous life experiences, getting my hopes up was the precursor to my dreams being crushed.

I vaguely heard Duke say goodbye and leave. I stayed in the office, playing the video over and over again while a thousand what-ifs ran through my head. There were so many things that could go wrong, injury being the first and foremost. It was a lot to consider, and I needed to get through the mess with Gabriella before I took on anything else.

I startled when I heard a knock on the office door. I glanced up to see Shaker's fine ass leaning against the door jamb. "Are you watching porn at work?"

I rolled my eyes, "Seriously?"

"What else would have you so fixated on the computer screen?" he asked with an arched brow.

I grinned, "Come here, and I'll show you."

Shaker closed the distance and stood behind me with his hands on my shoulders while I played the video for him. When it was over, he squeezed my shoulders gently, "Is that your horse?"

I snorted, "You sound like Duke. Yes, he's mine. His name is Blink."

"Blink?" he questioned.

"As in Blink of an Eye," I explained.

Shaker nodded, "Seems he lives up to his

name. I don't know as much about horses as you and Duke, but that seems like an impressive time to me."

"It is," I agreed.

"You don't sound very happy about that."

I sighed, feeling like the weight of the world was on my shoulders, "I am. It's just, I have a lot on my plate right now. I don't want to take on something this big while I have so many other irons in the fire."

"I'm not following. Take on what?" he asked.

"Oh, sorry. Racing Blink. It takes a lot of time and a lot of money, both of which I need to dedicate to Gabriella right now," I explained.

He smiled softly, "I think I can help with part of that."

I held my hands up as if to stop him. "No, I don't want your money."

He chuckled, "That's not what I meant. We had a meeting with Luke at the clubhouse today. He said the reason Hastings and Hensley were pushing for you to marry Preston was to get access to your trust fund; not the one you have access to now, but a different one. Did you know you had two?"

My eyes widened in shock. "Are you serious?"

"Yes. According to Luke, you would gain

access to it once you were married or turned 25 years old, whichever came first," he explained. "The lawyer should have contacted you once we were married."

"Shit!" I swore. "I haven't checked my PO Box in a few weeks."

"I can have one of the prospects go, if that's okay with you," he offered.

"Yeah, that would be great," I said, rummaging through my purse for the key. "Why would my mother leave me two trust funds?" I wondered out loud.

"I don't know, baby. Most people set up one and specify amounts to be released when certain stipulations are met. Could this one be from someone else?" he asked.

"I don't think so. My grandparents are the only other people who could possibly have established a trust fund for me, but there was no mention of it in their will," I explained.

"Let's see if there is anything in your box about it and go from there, yeah?" he asked.

"Sounds good," I agreed and handed him the key to my post office box.

Less than an hour later, Kellan arrived at the cottage with a box—yes, a box—of mail. I felt my cheeks heat with embarrassment. "Sorry, it's been a while since I've been out there to get my mail," I mumbled.

Kellan laughed, "You don't say."

"Oh, so you do have balls? Here I thought you were going to be a kiss ass forever," I snarked.

Kellan opened his mouth to reply, but Shaker beat him to it. "I'm going to stop this right here before it goes any further. Kellan, would you mind helping us go through her mail? We're specifically looking for anything that looks to be from a lawyer's office. And Keegan, play nice."

I rolled my eyes. "He knows I'm just messing with him. Right, Kellan?"

"Yes, ma'am."

I slapped a hand over my chest and dramatically stumbled backward. "Did you just *ma'am* me?"

Kellan laughed. "Sure did. See, I can be a smartass, too."

When his laughter died down, I shifted from foot to foot uncomfortably. "Kellan, um, I'm sorry for leaving yesterday and not telling you. Shaker filled me in on the details, and, well, I wanted to apologize as well as thank you for following me and getting word to the club. Yeah, Luke was involved, but none of us knew that, and if you hadn't been there...well, I'm thankful that you were."

His cheeks flushed, and he fixed his eyes on the box in his hands. "You're welcome. I'm glad everything turned out the way it did. So, should I just dump it?" he asked and wiggled the box of mail.

I shrugged, "Might as well. We can toss the envelopes back into the box as we're sorting."

"I think I found it," I exclaimed after well over half an hour of sorting. I ripped open the envelope and scanned the documents. "This has to be it. The letter asks me to contact the office in regards to my trust and inheritance from the Kensington Estate."

I looked over the letter and envelope again. "I don't think this is the same attorney that handled the trust fund I have access to now. Why would that be?" I wondered aloud.

Shaker shrugged, "Do you remember the other attorney's name?"

I shook my head, "No, but I have the name on the papers at my house."

"Do you want me to go get them for you?" Kellan offered.

"Thank you, but no. In the grand scheme of things, it doesn't really matter. It just seems odd is all," I answered.

Shaker's phone started buzzing on the coffee table. "Byte, what's up, brother?" he said by way of greeting. His eyes shot to me, and I suddenly felt unsettled. "Uh, yeah, I guess we can do that. Is everything okay?"

Kellan quickly got to his feet, his stance indicating he was ready for whatever Shaker might hand him.

"Okay, man, see you in a few. Thanks."

Shaker turned to me, concern filling his eyes, "We need to go to the clubhouse."

"Why?" Kellan and I asked at the same time.

"He didn't say. He just said he needed you and me to come to the clubhouse as soon as possible." He turned to Kellan, "Can you drive us there and back so we can avoid the hassle of the reporters?"

"Sure, man. I'm ready when you are," Kellan replied.

Kellan was driving one of the standard SUV's that belonged to the club and-or the farm. Even with the dark tint on the windows, Shaker insisted we duck down for the entirety of the trip to the clubhouse.

Upon arrival, Shaker and I were promptly escorted to Phoenix's office by Byte. I was surprised to find Ranger sitting in one of the chairs in front of Phoenix's desk. "Come on in and have a seat," Phoenix rumbled.

"Fine, but let's get on with it. You're kind of freaking me the hell out right now," I blurted and then slapped my hand over my mouth. "Sorry," I mumbled behind my fingers.

Phoenix laughed, "That's understandable given what you've been through recently, but we'll get right down to it. Byte, bring them up to speed."

Byte cleared his throat, "After the meeting with Luke, I was curious about the second trust fund mentioned, so I started poking around. To make a long story short, the trust fund you have access to now was started by your father. When he died, his life insurance money went into the trust and you were given access on your 18th birthday. The other trust fund is from your mother's side of the family."

I put my hand in the air, "Hold on just a second. My father? How do you know that? I don't even know who my father is," I said.

Byte looked confused. "What? But your parents were married."

"What?" I shrieked.

"Your parents were married. I have the marriage certificate pulled up right here," Byte said cautiously.

I felt tears stinging my eyes. Why would my mother keep that from me? I gasped, "I could have family out there. What's his name?"

Byte took a step back, and Phoenix stood. "That's why I asked you to come to the clubhouse. Byte recognized the name. Your father was Ranger's son, Kyle Norris," Phoenix said gently.

"The fuck you just say?" Ranger barked at the same time I shrieked another "What?"

Phoenix gestured to Byte, who turned the laptop so we could see the screen. There, in black and white, was a scanned document indicating that my mother did indeed marry a Kyle Quincy Norris almost a year before I was born. I looked to Ranger, "That's your son?"

His eyes were glistening as he nodded. "It is. Was. Damn it."

Phoenix clapped his hands together, "You two stay in here and chat. Everyone else, out."

"You okay, baby?" Shaker asked gently.

"Yeah, I'm good," I said, even though I wasn't sure that was true.

When the room cleared out, Ranger spoke again, "I didn't know about you. I knew he married a girl from Kentucky." He pinched the bridge of his nose and shook his head, "Kyle and

I had a falling out when he was around 19 years old. He took off and never looked back. I tried to keep up with him from a distance. He was still my boy. After he died, I didn't check up on his widow. It didn't even occur to me since I had never met the girl."

"I can't believe she never told me about him. They were married! Why would she keep that a secret? Why would she give me his middle name and not his last name? None of it makes any sense," I blurted.

"Your middle name is Quincy?" Ranger asked, looking surprised. I nodded. He smiled and held out his hand, "I'm Noah Quincy Norris. Nice to meet you."

I shook his hand and laughed, "I'm Keegan Quincy Kensington Marks. It's a pleasure to meet you as well."

"At least I have the answer to one thing that's been bugging the piss out of me," he grumbled.

"What's that?" I asked.

"Now I know why you're so good at playing pool," he deadpanned.

I burst out laughing. "That reminds me. I asked Shaker not to tell you, but given the circumstances, I'm going to tell you myself. So, that day when we played a few games of pool, that was the first time I'd played. Ever."

"That's not surprising. Well, not anymore. It's in your blood," he replied.

"So, um, is there more family?" I asked.

He shook his head, "Afraid not. My wife passed right before Kyle took off. He was our only child. My parents have long since passed, and my only brother died overseas serving our country. What about you?"

"I have a little sister, Gabriella. She's five years old. Mom died giving birth to her," I said, willing myself not to cry.

"I'm sorry to hear that. Where is the little one now?" he asked gently.

I scoffed, "Lawrence sent her away to boarding school. Luke is supposed to help me get full custody of her now that Lawrence has been arrested. As soon as I can, I will be bringing her back to Croftridge to live with me."

He patted my knee, "You let me know if you need any help with that."

"Thank you," I replied. "Um, what should I call you?"

"How about Ranger for now? I can't have people thinking I'm old enough to have a granddaughter your age."

"Hey now, I'm not that old," I huffed.

"No, you're not, but I'd have to be to have a grandkid your age," he stated flatly.

"Point made. Ranger it is," I laughed and rose to my feet.

Ranger grinned mischievously and held one finger against his lips in the universal be quiet sign. He took careful silent steps toward the door and reached for the doorknob. He gave a quick twist of his wrist and a firm shove to the door. I distinctly heard two loud thumps followed by "Ow!" and "Hey!"

Ranger pushed the door open and said to Kellan and Shaker, "Let that be a lesson to you, you nosy little fucks."

CHAPTER TWENTY-TWO

Shaker

Keegan was taking everything in stride. I kept watching and waiting for her to breakdown, but it never happened. She spent her mornings at the barn, but came back to the cottage to spend her afternoons tending to her personal business, which mainly consisted of phone calls to lawyers and a few to Luke. We spent the evenings together, just like any other married couple, both of us avidly avoiding the elephant in the room.

I was struggling with my emotions, as well as my physical needs as a man. I was painfully hard any time I was in the same room with her and half the time when I wasn't. I needed a release, and I needed it before I lost my damn mind. We had been at the cottage a little over a week, and I hadn't touched her since the first day we were there. It felt wrong to engage in anything sexual with her until we discussed our future plans.

Right on cue, as if things weren't hard enough for me already, Keegan entered the kitchen wrapped only in a towel. I sucked in a sharp breath causing her to whirl around.

"Sorry," she shrugged and gulped down a glass of water. "I got really thirsty in the shower."

"I need a shower," I gritted out and stalked to the bathroom to take care of my issue. I tossed my shirt to the floor and started undoing my belt when I noticed Keegan coming up behind me. She pressed her towel-clad body against my back and ran her hands from my chest, down my stomach, to my very noticeable erection.

I grabbed her hands and stopped her. "We can't do this," I said.

She rolled her eyes at me, "Not this shit, again."

"I'm serious, Keegan. We need to talk first," I said, ignoring her snide comment.

She huffed, "Fine. What is it we need to talk about right this minute?"

"Us," I said softly. "It feels wrong to do

this without talking about the future of our relationship."

"You didn't seem to mind before," she retorted.

"I'll admit I got caught up in the moment several times. I guess it seems different now that there's an end in sight," I explained.

"Okay, so, what? You don't want to have sex now?" she asked.

I laughed sardonically, "Baby, with you, wanting to has never been an issue."

She pinned me with her gaze, hands firmly on her hips, "I'm not going to try to guess whatever it is you're trying to say. Spit. It. Out."

"Do you want to be in a relationship with me?" I blurted, sounding like a complete and total pussy.

A surprised look washed over her face for a brief moment before she masked it. "We're married. I think that qualifies as a relationship."

I sighed, "That was fake, and you know it. I meant a real relationship."

She gave me a pitying look, "Aww, did you go and catch feelings?"

I threw my hands in the air, "Fuck this shit!" I turned to storm out when three words stopped me in my tracks.

"I love you," she said firmly.

I whirled around, "Say it again."

"I love you," she repeated without hesitation.

It was the balm my broken soul needed to heal. I closed the distance between us and cupped her face in my hands, "I love you, too, baby."

"Good. Now shut up and kiss me."

I tugged on her bottom lip with my teeth. "Oh, I'm going to do more than kiss you."

With that, I yanked the towel from her body and turned her around to face the mirror. "Hands on the counter," I told her while I shoved my jeans down my legs and kicked them into the corner of the room.

Reaching into the drawer, I grabbed a condom and quickly smoothed it down my shaft. When I looked up, Keegan was intently watching my every move. I stepped forward, nestling my cock in the crack of her ass, and reached around to cup her breasts.

Pulling her flush against my chest, I captured her nipple between my thumb and forefinger while my other hand slid down her stomach to cup her sex. "Watch," I breathed against her ear.

Her eyes met mine in the mirror for a brief second before they darted to my hand teasing her nipple. When I used one finger to trace the seam of her slick slit, her eyes moved to the juncture of her thighs, and she pressed back against me.

"You like that?" I asked with my mouth still pressed against her ear.

"Yes," she moaned.

"Spread your legs for me," I instructed as I moved my hand to her other breast.

She immediately complied, and I slowly slid one finger inside while massaging her clit with my thumb. "Jacob, I'm about to come," she said, almost sounding panicked, but I knew why. She preferred to come while I was inside of her.

"Watching me toy with your nipples and glide my fingers through your wet little pussy really got you worked up, didn't it, wifey?"

She started panting and trying to squirm out of my hold. "Fuck, yes, you know it did," she said, and her eyes began to close.

"Keep watching, and I'll give you what you want."

Her eyes flew open and fixated on the spot between her thighs. I removed my fingers from her heat and positioned myself at her entrance. I met her gaze in the mirror as I slowly entered her, not stopping until I was buried as deep as I could go.

And that was it for Keegan's patience. She slapped her hands onto the counter and pushed back with determination. With one hand gripping her hip and one wrapped around her jaw, I met her thrust for thrust. When her lips parted, and her eyes widened, I knew she was about to explode.

I pulled out, turned her around, hoisted her up onto the counter, and slid right back into place in a matter of seconds. Wrapping my arms around her, I covered her mouth with mine and continued to move as we reached our climaxes together.

Pressing soft kisses to her lips, I requested, "Say it again."

She smiled. "I love you."

"Yeah, I love you, too, wifey."

We cleaned up, and I followed her to the bedroom. Once we were settled, I asked, "Do you think we should stay married?"

"I think it would be stupid to get divorced so we could start dating. If word got out, we would have a lot of explaining to do. Besides, it was you who suggested we stay married until I have full custody of Gabriella," she replied.

"How is that going, by the way?" I asked.

"Good. Great actually. Lawrence signed the

papers. He refused at first, but Luke was able to convince him otherwise. He still wasn't happy about it," she explained.

"If he signed the papers, why haven't you gone to get her yet?" I asked. I figured she would have been on her way to get her sister the second the ink hit the papers.

"It's not that simple. He isn't signing over custody to me, per se. He's agreeing to voluntarily terminate his parental rights and giving consent to adopt. The family court lawyer said adoption would be the best route to take. A judge has to review the case and approve the order before I can go get her," she explained.

She suddenly shot up in bed and covered her mouth with both hands. "Oh, no. I'm so stupid. I have to call Luke," she blurted and reached to grab her phone.

I gently tugged her by her wrist to get her attention. "What's going on? Talk to me."

She turned to me with wide, panicked eyes and started to cry. "I can't adopt her because we're married," she wailed.

"Fuck. Because of the club," I mused.

She wiped her nose with the back of her hand and shook her head. "No, it doesn't have anything to do with the club."

"Keegan, baby, tell me what the problem is," I said, not bothering to hide my frustration.

"Okay, okay," she said while bobbing her head. She wiped the tears from her cheeks and sniffled. "We're married, so *I* can't adopt her. *We* can, but *I* can't."

She wasn't telling me anything I didn't already know. "The problem, Keegan. Tell me the problem."

She tilted her head to the side and stared at me. Then, she closed her eyes and dropped her chin to her chest. She shook her head and whispered, "I won't ask this of you."

Realization dawned and I reached for her. "You don't have to ask. I love you, and I want to help you get your sister. And, yes, I know that means adopting her with you. If things don't work out with us, I wouldn't try to take her away from you. Don't forget, your grandfather is also a Blackwing. I may be an officer, but he's an original member. The club won't let anyone take her from you, not even me."

"This is a big deal, Jacob," she whispered against my shoulder.

"Yeah, it is. It's also the right thing to do. You and I both know that."

"Thank you," she said with a wobbly voice.

"Do you have any idea when your case will go before a judge?" I asked.

"My lawyer and Luke were trying to get things expedited for me. I'm hoping everything will be finalized by the end of next week, but you never know with the judicial system."

"Let me know about any appointments or meetings. Doesn't matter what they are, I want to go with you," I said.

"You're an amazing man," she smiled sweetly and placed a soft kiss to my lips. "When do you think we can go home?"

"Ember said there had been a steady decline in the number of reporters at the gate each day. Phoenix said the same for the clubhouse. I'm guessing we should be able to leave here after a few more days. 'Home' as in your house?"

"Well, yeah. Where else would we live?" she asked incredulously.

I shrugged, "I don't know. We could get a new place. Something a little bigger for when your sister comes to live with us."

"Let's give the dust some time to settle before we go stirring up more, yeah?" she said carefully.

"Okay, wifey," I agreed and pecked her lips. "Let's get some sleep."

***

I was right; we were able to return to Keegan's house within a few days. Once there, we spent our evenings preparing a room for Gabriella. Keegan wanted her transition to living with us to be as smooth as possible. Personally, I thought she was worried about the upcoming court date and needed to stay busy to keep her sanity. When I asked her about it, she completely denied the possibility.

The weekend before the court date, we headed back to Kentucky. Keegan managed to get access to Lawrence's house in order to pack up any of Gabriella's belongings as well as any of their mother's items that held sentimental value. Keegan was dead set against bringing any furniture from the senator's house into hers. Since we rented a box truck to move Gabriella's things, I suggested we go ahead and shop for her bedroom furniture.

Keegan found what she wanted at a furniture store in the downtown area. After we loaded the furniture into the truck, we stopped to have lunch before going to Lawrence's house. The server had just returned with our drinks and taken our order when I heard a voice from my past, a voice I never thought I would—nor wanted to—ever hear again.

"Well, if it isn't Jacob Marks," Beth's nasally, shrill voice sounded from behind me.

I visibly cringed and tried to swallow down the bile forcing its way up my throat. I closed my eyes and took a deep breath before acknowledging the bitch of all bitches. I slightly turned in my seat toward the speaking demon, "Hello, Beth."

She sauntered up to the table, swaying her hips in an exaggerated fashion. "Hello, Jacob," she said breathily. "It's so good to see you." She turned to give Keegan a once over, "And who's this?"

Keegan straightened in her seat and squared her shoulders. "His wife," she snapped.

Beth laughed, "Oh, that's right. I heard about your nuptials. Honestly, I thought it was a rumor." She glanced at Keegan again, then down to her hand. Her eyes shot to me, and an evil grin appeared on her face before it morphed into one of surprise. She gasped and glanced between Keegan's face and mine, "You gave her my rings?"

Keegan tried to hide the hurt on her face, but I saw it, and Beth did, too, before she was able to mask it. Keegan yanked her hand into her lap and glared at me. "What do you want, Beth?" I barked.

"I just wanted to come over and say hello to my ex-fiancé," she replied sweetly.

I rose to my feet, "I was never your fiancé, and you know it."

"You bought those rings for me," she replied.

"No, I bought those rings for the woman I thought you were before I found out you were nothing but a lying, cheating, gold-digging whore," I spat.

Beth twirled a piece of her hair around her finger, "Are you still mad about the baby?"

I looked at her, really looked at her, and suddenly realized I was playing right into her hands. She wanted to stir up trouble and cause a scene, and I was making it easy for her. I smiled like a psycho and stared at her in silence for several beats. "Of course not. I'm upset with you for disturbing my lunch with my beautiful wife." I raised my hand beside my head and snapped my fingers. Kellan appeared at my side almost instantly. "Please take out the trash," I said.

"Gladly," Kellan said, grabbing Beth by her shoulders. "Let's go."

Beth shrieked and started yelling, "Get your hands off of me! Someone, call the police!" She was fighting Kellan every step of the way. I guess he had enough of it because, in the next second, he hoisted Beth over his shoulder and marched out the front door as he announced, "No need for concern. Just a little lovers' quarrel."

I dropped back into my chair to find a set of wedding rings on my plate and no Keegan in sight. Fucking Beth. I sighed and tried to figure out how I was going to fix this mess. I sent a text to Kellan and told him where to meet me; then I paid for our uneaten meal before heading to my next stop.

CHAPTER TWENTY-THREE

Keegan

To say I was mad would not be an accurate statement. I was furious, for a number of reasons. Reason numero uno, some two-bit hussy publicly claimed that the wedding rings on my finger were hers. Reason number two, Shaker's past included a fiancée. A fiancée I knew nothing about.

It was only a matter of time before he showed up at Lawrence's house, so I was trying to pack and get out of there as fast as possible. I didn't want to talk to him, not yet anyway. Unfortunately, I heard him enter the house less than an hour after I had arrived. He didn't call out to me, and I didn't volunteer my location.

Lawrence's house was huge; it would take him several minutes to find me and even longer if I was hiding. With that thought, I tiptoed over to Gabriella's huge toy box filled with stuffed animals and buried myself inside.

After about five minutes, I felt like an idiot for hiding from Shaker. I was a mature adult and should just tell him I was upset and not ready to talk about it yet. Surely, he would understand and give me some space. I started to climb out of the toy box when I heard a voice that decidedly did not belong to Shaker.

"Keep looking! She's in here somewhere," Lois Hensley hissed.

Panic gripped me. Who was she talking to? How did she know where I was? More importantly, why was she looking for me?

"Keep your voice down, Mom. We don't want her to hear us," Preston whispered harshly.

Shit! Motherfucking pile of giant cow shit!

"Looks like she's been in this room," Lois said, sounding much closer than she had before. Where was Shaker? I felt my pockets for my phone, hoping I could manage to send a text to him when I remembered turning it off and tossing it on the passenger seat of the box truck.

I tried to keep myself still and breathe

as quietly as possible. It was getting harder and harder each second. The stuffed animals weren't exactly breathable, and it was getting uncomfortably hot. I needed to hold out until Shaker arrived. I had no idea what Lois and Preston wanted with me, but I knew it couldn't be anything good.

Searing pain shot through my scalp as I was yanked from the toy box by my hair and unceremoniously dropped onto the floor. When I looked up, I came face to face with the barrel of a gun. "Stand up, bitch," Lois ordered.

I held my hands up in surrender and slowly rose to my feet. I couldn't hide the tremor in my voice when I asked, "Why are you doing this?"

"You know damn well why I'm doing this. You have ruined everything for me. The least I can do is return the favor," she spat.

I needed to keep her talking. I had always heard that, keep them talking so you can try to find a way out or wait for help to arrive. "What did I ruin, Lois?"

She scoffed, "You can't be that stupid. It's because of you my husband will probably spend the rest of his life in prison. You tarnished my son's reputation, my family's reputation. And you destroyed my income!"

I couldn't help myself. My resolve to stay calm flew out the window with her accusations. "Are you serious right now? I didn't have anything to do with your husband going to prison. The FBI was investigating him and Lawrence well before they decided to kidnap and sell me. As for your son, he's the one who thought he could get away with sexually assaulting me. And I can't even begin to process your comment about your income. You are a woman, and you're pissed off about losing income generated by trafficking women? You are one twisted bitch," I yelled.

Her face turned damn near purple with anger. "Shut up! Just shut up!" she screamed.

Pop.

Pain exploded in my chest.

Pop.

The pain in my chest expanded to my stomach.

Pop.

Everything faded away.

CHAPTER TWENTY-FOUR

Shaker

I had a bad feeling, and it had nothing to do with Keegan being upset with me. No, this was different. A deep, piercing sense of dread consumed me.

"You all right, man?" Kellan asked from the driver's seat.

"Not really. Something's not right. I can feel it," I said quietly.

Kellan didn't comment or ask any other questions, but I did feel the car accelerate as he tried to get us to the Hastings estate faster.

When we pulled up to the house, the reason for my dread was painfully obvious. A familiar car was parked beside the box truck we rented.

"Fuck! That's Preston's car," I barked, climbing out of Kellan's cage and reaching for my gun.

We ran to the house with our guns drawn. The front door was wide open. I cautiously, but quickly, entered the house. My eyes frantically searched for Preston or Keegan.

Pop.

Pop.

Pop.

Oh, fuck no. Gunshots. I knew beyond a shadow of a doubt Keegan wasn't armed. Without thought for my own well-being, I sprinted toward the sound. I could hear Kellan's footfalls behind me. We ran down a long hallway and rounded the corner to find Lois Hensley with a gun trained on Keegan and Preston Hensley with a gun trained on me.

I didn't wait. I didn't speak. I didn't think. I just did. I fired one shot at Lois, a small, dark hole appearing on her forehead. I quickly turned to fire at Preston to find him already on the ground with a matching bullet hole on his own forehead.

Dropping to my knees beside Keegan, I placed my fingers against her neck and prayed for a pulse. It was faint, but it was there. "We need an ambulance and the police at the Hastings estate.

The senator's stepdaughter has been shot," I heard Kellan saying behind me.

"I need help, man!" I yelled. He dropped his phone and knelt beside me. "Hold pressure on her stomach. I've got her chest."

We stayed like that, desperately trying to stanch the blood that continued to pour out of her limp body. Her breaths were becoming more and more shallow while her skin grew paler with each passing minute. "Where the fuck are they?" I bellowed.

"Right here. Please move aside so we can help her," a paramedic said.

"We can't let go. She's already lost too much blood," Kellan explained.

The paramedic gathered some items and moved in beside me, sliding his hands underneath mine. I noticed another paramedic doing the same thing with Kellan. As soon as our hands were free, we took a few steps back. I couldn't take my eyes off Keegan.

"Place your hands on your head and slowly turn around. Then, lower yourself to your knees. Both of you," a booming voice called out.

I whirled around with my hands in the air. "You have got to be fucking kidding me right now!" I roared. "My wife is dying, and you're trying to arrest me?!"

"I won't ask again," the cop yelled.

"Shaker, cooperate. They'll get it sorted," Kellan pleaded.

"Fuck that!" I turned to check on my wife, and white-hot pain surged through me from head to toe. Every muscle in my body contracted and felt like it was on fire. I fell to the floor convulsing, trying to figure out what had happened to me.

What felt like an eternity later, my muscles relaxed, and my brain started to come back online. I was still on the floor, now on my stomach with my hands cuffed behind my back. My eyes searched the room, but there was no sign of Keegan, other than the profuse amount of her blood staining the floor.

I fixated on the large pool of blood in the center of the room. My wife's blood. Too much of my wife's blood for her to be alive. I closed my eyes and choked back the sob trying to force its way out.

"Get him up and get him to the station," an unfamiliar voice said.

"No! Please! Let me see my wife! Where is she?" I asked as I frantically scanned the room for Keegan.

"They took her to the hospital," Kellan said

quietly from my side.

"When did they take her?" I asked, still feeling like I was in a fog.

"Right after they tasered you for resisting arrest," he answered.

"No!" I roared and futilely yanked against the handcuffs. "I have to get to the hospital. You have to let me go. You have it all wrong!"

The cop snorted sardonically, "Like we haven't heard that before."

"Let them go." Relief filled me at the sound of a familiar and friendly voice.

"And why would I do that?" the cop asked.

Luke entered the room and flashed his badge. "I'm Luke Johnson. This is part of an open federal investigation in which I am the lead agent. In other words, because I said so," Luke retorted.

"I can't just release two murder suspects," the cop said.

"Release them now, or I'll have your badge," Luke barked. "Did you even ask them what happened before you cuffed them?"

"I didn't have the opportunity to ask them anything. That one there," he said, pointing to me, "became aggressive and resisted arrest."

"Oh, really? Or was he distraught over his

wife's condition?" Luke questioned. "Uncuff. Them. Now."

The cop huffed and gestured for his partner to release us. As the cuffs were coming off, Luke said, "I have a car waiting downstairs to take you to the hospital. I'll meet you there when I finish up here."

"Thanks, Luke," I managed to choke out as Kellan and I ran toward the waiting car.

I called my mother on the way to the hospital. If anyone, other than Keegan, would be able to help me keep my shit together, it was my mother.

"I called Phoenix and filled him in. He's going to get Ranger, and they'll be on their way," Kellan said.

I clapped him on the shoulder to say thanks, and he winced. I jerked my hand back and saw blood staining my fingers. "Shit, Kellan. You got hit?"

"Yeah. It's not a big deal. I'll have it looked at after we find out how Keegan is doing," he said.

I shook my head. "No, brother, you'll have it looked at as soon as we get there. Keegan is probably already in surgery, and we won't know anything for a while." I felt like shit for thinking it, but in a way, Kellan getting shot gave me something to focus on until there was news about Keegan.

When we arrived at the hospital, Kellan was immediately taken back to a room. I stopped at the desk and asked about Keegan. I was right; she was in surgery, which meant she was still alive. I made sure my phone number was attached to her chart and told the woman where I could be found. I also asked her to call me when my mother arrived, and yes, I shamelessly name-dropped.

Her eyes widened at the mention of my mother. "Yes, Mr. Marks. I will call right away. I'm going to call my supervisor and see about arranging a private waiting room for you while your wife is in surgery. Is there anything else I can do to be of help?" she asked.

"That will be all for now. Thank you," I replied and tapped the counter twice. I didn't care for this part of the wealthy lifestyle. Everyone was overly eager to get on your good side and seemed to be constantly kissing your ass. However, in the current situation, I would take anything I could get if it would help Keegan.

I walked back to Kellan's room to find him being stitched up by a guy who looked far too young to be working in a hospital, much less to be a physician. "How is she?" Kellan asked when he saw me enter the room.

"She's in surgery. That's all I know," I muttered. I jerked my chin toward his shoulder, "How's the arm?"

"It'll be fine. It was a clean through and through. When the doc is finished sewing me up, I'll be good to go," Kellan replied, sounding bored.

A few minutes later, I heard a commotion coming from the other side of the door that led to the Emergency Department's waiting room. I grinned, "Sounds like my mother has arrived."

The doctor's head shot up, and he looked me over, "Who is your mother?"

The door opened, and she answered, "I am."

"Mrs. Marks, it's a pleasure to see you again, though I hope unpleasant circumstances are not the reason for your visit today," the doctor babbled. See? Constant ass kissing. My mother was on the board of directors for the hospital and also donated an obscene amount of money to the hospital each year. Of course, everyone in the place knew who she was and would try to please her in any way they could.

My mother gestured toward Kellan, "Obviously, that is exactly why I am here." She turned her attention to me, "Are you all right, sweetheart? How is Keegan?"

I pulled my mother in for a hug. "I'm okay, physically. Keegan is in surgery, but I don't know, Mom, it was bad," I choked out, not bothering to fight the tears welling in my eyes.

"Oh, baby," my mother soothed. "She's a strong girl, and this hospital is home to some of the best surgeons in the country. We'll wait, and we'll pray, and we'll stay strong for Keegan."

We were taken to a private waiting room when Kellan was discharged from the Emergency Department. Luke arrived not long after we had gotten settled. He offered to take our statements later, but I needed the distraction. Time was crawling at a snail's pace, and it was only a matter of time before I lost control of myself.

We were almost finished talking to Luke when Phoenix and what looked like the majority of the original chapter of the Blackwings MC arrived. Ranger came stomping over and interrupted without giving a single shit. "Where is my grandbaby?" he demanded.

"She's still in surgery," I replied.

He nodded and eyed Kellan. Jerking his chin toward his shoulder, he asked, "What happened to you, Prospect?"

"I was shot, sir," Kellan answered.

"Defending my granddaughter?"

"He shot Preston while I shot Lois. Preston got a shot off before he went down," I answered for Kellan.

Ranger nodded and turned to Phoenix, "No disrespect, but you need to patch this boy in. He's saved my granddaughter a few times over now. As far as I'm concerned, he's more than earned it."

"I agree with Ranger, Prez. No disrespect here either," I said.

Phoenix laughed, "I was planning on calling for a vote on him as soon as your damn dust settled, Shaker."

"Oh, well, okay then," I mumbled. Ranger nodded in agreement.

Luke cleared his throat, "I need to get back to the office. I think I have everything I need from the two of you for now. I'll need to get Keegan's statement when she's awake and ready. Jacquelyn, may I speak with you for a moment?"

My mother gracefully rose and followed Luke into the hallway. A few moments later, she returned sans Luke and said, "There is a small issue that requires my attention. I will be back as soon as possible. Call me if there's any news." She kissed me on the cheek and disappeared with her head of security, Ronan, on her heels.

"She's up to something," I said, more to myself than anyone else.

I found a seat and dropped my head into my hands. I had no idea how long we would have to wait before we heard something about Keegan. I let out a heavy breath and tried to rein in my emotions, but I was struggling.

A soft hand landed on my shoulder, and I turned my head to find Harper sitting beside me. She reached over and clasped my hand in hers. Then, she repeated the words I said to her right after we escaped from the hidden house in the hills. "Not yet. If you lose it, I'll lose it, and we can't do that right now. Got me?"

Squeezing her hand, I whispered, "Got you."

I have no idea how long we waited before the door opened, and a male voice said, "Family of Keegan Marks?"

Ranger and I were on our feet and in front of the man in a flash. "How is she?" we both barked out at the same time.

I'll give the man credit; he didn't so much as flinch in response to our gruff tone. What unnerved me was the unreadable mask on his face. "Let's step out into the hall," he said and didn't wait for us to agree or disagree.

He started talking about her injuries and what they did to repair them. He was talking and talking but only a few words registered to me— two gunshot wounds to the chest, one gunshot wound to the abdomen, collapsed lung, fractured sternum, couldn't save the kidney. He kept going and going, and I couldn't take it anymore. "Just tell me if she's alive!" I bellowed.

He blinked stupidly and slowly said, "Yes, she's alive. She's in critical condition, but she is still with us."

I sagged in relief at his words. Ranger's big paw landed on my shoulder, "Go have a seat, brother. I'll finish up with the doctor."

"No. I want to see her," I stated.

"You can, as soon as she is moved to a room," the doctor replied automatically.

"No, I want to see her now," I demanded.

"Sir—" he started to protest.

"My name is Mr. Marks," I said. "Mr. Jacob Kingsley Marks."

"As in?"

"Yes, as in those Marks. Now, may I please see my wife?" I asked desperately.

"We usually have the family wait until the patient has been moved to a room, but I think we can make an exception in this case. Please follow me," he said.

Ranger stayed in step with me, and I didn't question it. After all, he was her only living blood relative besides her younger sister. Yes, I was her husband, but if it hadn't been for the fucked up circumstances, we wouldn't be married.

The doctor led us through a set of double doors. I was immediately accosted with the harsh chemical smell only found in hospitals. Machines were beeping, phones were ringing, and people were buzzing about. It was almost too much for me to stand at that moment. Then, my eyes landed on Keegan.

She was so pale and so still. She had tubes and wires coming from her face, her arms, and from underneath her blankets. I gingerly placed a kiss on her forehead and slid my hand underneath hers. Ranger followed suit, kissing the top of her head, then smoothing his hand over her hair.

"Keegan, baby, if you can hear me, you have to fight. I need you. Gabriella needs you. And Ranger needs you. So, you have to stay strong and fight to get through this," I choked out.

"He's right, sweetheart. I just got you, and I'm not ready to give you up," Ranger croaked.

They let us stay with her until it was time

to move her to a room. Ranger and I returned to the waiting room and updated everyone. I called my mother as she requested, but she didn't answer her phone. I knew she wanted to know about Keegan, so I called Ronan's phone. No answer. What the hell? I frowned at my phone in confusion.

"Something wrong?" Phoenix asked.

"I'm not sure," I muttered. "My mother isn't answering her phone, and neither is her head of security."

"Give me their phone numbers, and I'll try to get in touch with them. You have enough to worry about right now."

Hours passed before I finally heard from my mother. She assured me everything was okay but said she wouldn't be able to get back to the hospital until the next day. She had, however, had time to arrange for Keegan to be placed in a large private suite with two cots for Ranger and I. My mother was truly amazing. She also booked hotel rooms near the hospital for the club members. Only two questions remained, where was she and what was she doing?

CHAPTER TWENTY-FIVE

Keegan

Everything hurt. It felt like my entire body was one big bruise. My mind felt foggy, and something was scratching the hell out of my throat. I tried to open my eyes, but they wouldn't open. I heard a rhythmic sound of something whooshing and whirring nearby. There were other strange sounds around me, but I drifted back into oblivion before I could give it much more thought.

When I came around again, it seemed lighter beyond my eyelids. I tried again to force the little shits open, but they refused to cooperate. Why couldn't I open my eyes, and why did I hurt so bad? I opened my mouth to ask just that, but nothing came out. I tried again. This time, a low moan was all I was able to produce. What was wrong with me? I started to get scared and tried to force my body to move. Instead of cooperating, my body was overwrought with a searing pain from my neck to my chest. I heard a female voice in the distance say, "She's okay. I'm going to give her something for the breakthrough pain. She'll settle down in just a moment." She was right; the blackness consumed me moments later.

A familiar cry brought pulled me from the darkness. "Sissy!" Gabriella cried. Wait. Gabriella? With every bit of strength I could muster, I forced my eyes open. It was not the greatest feeling in the world. They were dry and scratchy, and everything was blurry. I could see figures and shadows, but that was about it. "Slowly blink a few times, dear," a soft feminine voice said. I knew that voice. Jacquelyn.

I followed her instructions and blinked several times until my vision magically cleared. Jacquelyn was standing beside me with my baby sister perched on her hip. I opened my mouth to speak, but only a hissed whisper sound came out. "Don't try to talk just yet, dear. Let me call the nurse and let her know you're awake."

Seconds later, a nurse briskly entered the

room and started checking things. She allowed me to have a few sips of water, and let me tell you, that was the best damn water in the world. She smiled kindly, "Are you in any pain?"

"A little," I answered. "What happened?"

"You don't remember?" she asked.

"No, I don't."

"I'll tell her," a deep, male voice said and stepped into my line of sight. Shaker. He stepped closer and picked up my hand, holding it between both of his. "Baby, you were shot, three times to be exact."

At his words, it all came flooding back. Lois. Preston. The pain hitting my chest. I shuddered and felt tears pooling in my eyes. "I remember," I whispered. Then, a thought suddenly occurred to me. "It was Lois Hensley. Preston was there, too."

He nodded. "I know. Kellan and I were coming through the front door when we heard the gunshots."

"Did you catch them?" I asked, hopefully.

He rubbed the back of his neck, "Uh, yeah, I guess you could say that." He glanced behind him and leaned in closer to my ear. "We killed them, baby," he whispered and leaned back.

"Oh, good. Thank you," I said.

He laughed, "Thank you, she says. That's classic."

Jacquelyn cleared her throat, "I have a little wiggle worm here who has been waiting patiently to see her big sister."

Shaker smiled and took Gabriella from Jacquelyn's arms. He met her eyes and asked, "Do you remember what we talked about?"

She nodded firmly. "Yes, I do. I have to be very gentle, and I can only touch her arms or her face. I can do it. I promise."

Shaker nodded once and sat her on the bed at my side facing me. "Hey, Gabriella," I said softly. "How did you get here?"

"My long, lost fairy grandmother brought me here," she said, smiling from ear to ear. "And guess what else! I have a long, lost grandfather, too!"

"You do?" I asked, completely confused and wondering if it had anything to do with the medication I had been receiving.

"That'd be me. Hope that's okay," Ranger said, appearing out of nowhere. "I figured since I was yours, I might as well be hers, too."

"I thought you didn't want anyone knowing you were a grandfather," I smiled.

"To someone your age," he shot back. "This

one right here is fine." He smoothed Gabriella's hair and grinned.

"Gabriella, how about your Papa and I take you to get something to eat? We'll come back and see Keegan before going back to the hotel tonight," Jacquelyn asked.

Gabriella beamed at Jacquelyn, "Yay! I'll be back, Sissy. Love you."

Jacquelyn scooped Gabriella from the bed and propped her on her hip. "I thought you two might like to have a few minutes to yourselves before everyone else gets back from dinner."

"Everyone else?" I asked.

"Most of the club is here, baby," Shaker answered.

"See you in a bit, sweetheart," Ranger said and placed a kiss on top of my head. With that, he followed Jacquelyn and Gabriella out of the room.

Shaker sat in a chair beside the bed and carefully lifted my hand to his lips before letting it rest in his hand on the bed. "I love you, Keegan. I've never been so fucking scared in my entire life when I saw you on the floor, blood pooling underneath you..." he trailed off, and I thought I heard a hitch in his voice.

"Jacob," I said softly.

He lifted his head and met my eyes; one single tear slid down his cheek. "I can't lose you," he croaked.

"You won't," I said, trying to reassure him.

"I'm sorry about before. You know, about what happened at the restaurant. She was never my fiancée, and she never wore those rings. I don't know how she even knew about them. Still, I never should have given them to you, fake marriage or not," he said.

"No, I completely overreacted to the situation. I should've given you a chance to explain," I said.

"I should have at least told you where I got the rings before we got married," he mumbled.

"It's okay. Like I said, I overreacted. Things have changed between us since—"

The door pushed open, and a sea of leather flowed in, with Harper leading the crowd. "Keegan!" she squealed. She leaned in and gave me a gentle hug. "I'm so happy you're awake. We've been so worried. How are you feeling?"

I smiled at her rapid-fire questions. "I'm okay right now. They gave me some medicine for the pain not that long ago, so I don't know how much longer I'll be coherent."

One by one, the club brothers and their women circled through the room to greet me.

It reminded me of the receiving line at our reception. I was amazed at how many of them had come. It wasn't like I was a 30-minute drive away in Cedar Valley; I was in a hospital an entire state away.

Duke was the last one in line. "Don't worry about the barn. I'll take care of things until you're back on your feet."

"I can't ask you to do that. It'll be months before I can work at the barn," I said solemnly.

"You'll be able to sit and give orders to the prospects in just a few weeks. Plus, we have that new stable hand to help out," he said with a smile.

"Thanks, Duke," I said sincerely.

By the time the club left, as well as Jacquelyn, Gabriella, and Ranger, I was exhausted. I turned my tired eyes to Shaker, "Can we finish our conversation tomorrow? I don't think I can keep my eyes open much longer."

"Sleep, baby. I'll be here when you wake up."

CHAPTER TWENTY-SIX

Shaker

After Keegan fell asleep, I pulled the new rings from my pocket and carefully slipped them on the third finger of her left hand. I bought them after our run-in with Beth before going to Lawrence's house. I hadn't planned on giving them to her this way, but after everything that happened, it seemed like the right thing to do. Having to wait for her to notice them was going to kill me.

I didn't have to wait long. She noticed first thing the next morning. "What in the hell is this, Jacob Kingsley Marks?" she screeched, waving her hand in the air.

"What does it look like, Keegan Quincy

Kensington Marks?" I shot right back.

She pinned me with a glare and arched an eyebrow. I sighed and gave her what she wanted. "I bought you your own rings like I should have done in the first place," I said, pausing for a moment. "That's why I didn't get to Lawrence's house sooner. I'm so sorry, Keegan."

"Wait a second. You don't think this is your fault, do you?" she asked carefully.

"If I had gotten there sooner—" I started, but she cut me off.

"Stop right there. I'm not letting you do this. Lois and Preston are the only ones to blame for my injuries. Well, I suppose Lawrence and Harold deserve some of the blame, too. But you, none of this is your fault. If you had gotten there sooner, they might have gotten away and then killed one or both of us later. So, we are NOT playing the blame game, and we are NOT playing the what if game. Do you understand me?"

I simply nodded. What could I say to that?

"I need words," she growled.

I smiled, "I understand."

"So, we're doing this?" she asked.

"Yeah, baby, we're doing this."

Keegan spent over two weeks in the hospital. Ranger, Gabriella, and my mother were at her side every day. When she was finally discharged, she wanted to go home to Croftridge, but I didn't think she would be able to handle riding in a car for that length of time. When she started to argue with me, my mother held up her hand and told us she would take care of it. An hour later, the five of us were flying to Croftridge in a private jet chartered by my mother.

When we turned onto our street, Keegan cleared her throat to get my attention. Her furrowed brow and wrinkled nose had me instantly on alert. "What's wrong?"

"I want to see Gabriella when she sees her room, but I haven't talked to her about living with us yet," she whispered.

"Okay, so let's get you settled on the couch or in bed, and then you can talk to her. When you're ready to show her the room, I'll take you in there first, then go back and bring her in," I suggested.

"Thank you. Will, um, will you stay with me when I tell her?"

"Of course, I will," I assured her as we pulled into the driveway.

With Keegan propped up in our oversized chair in the living room, I placed Gabriella beside her and took a seat on the ottoman next to Keegan's feet. My mother and Ranger were in the kitchen giving us the privacy we needed, but ready to swoop in and help if things didn't go well.

"Gabriella, what did Father tell you about the school you went to?" Keegan asked, and I could tell it disgusted her to refer to Lawrence as Father, but it was what Gabriella called him.

"He said I had to go because he was away a lot. I didn't want to go. He said I was a cry baby and made me go anyway. I hate it there. Do I have to go back?" Gabriella blurted.

Keegan smiled. "Well, Father is going to be away for a long time, and little girls can't live all alone—"

"Sissy! Can I live with you?" Gabriella asked excitedly and moved to launch herself at Keegan, but I caught her just as her little body started to leap. "I want to live with you and Shaky Jakey!"

Keegan grabbed a pillow and held it against her chest as she tried not to laugh. "With who?"

Gabriella shot her big sister an incredulous look, then pointed at me with her thumb. "Him. Papa said his nickname was Shaky Jakey."

Ranger's rumbled laughter filtered out from the kitchen. "Oh, he did, did he?"

"Can I? Can I can I can I can I can I can I??

Pleeeeeease?" Gabriella begged.

Keegan nodded with tears in her eyes "Yes, sweet girl, you can."

"Why you crying, Sissy?"

"Because you want to live with us. These are happy tears," Keegan explained.

"We have a surprise for you, little miss. Go in the kitchen with Grammy and Papa while we get it ready for you," I said as I set her on her feet.

"You got it, Shaky Jakey."

"Your grandfather is going to pay for that," I grumbled as I lifted Keegan into my arms and carried her down the hall to Gabriella's room.

"I like it," the smartass said.

Instead of trying to get her situated on the tiny bed, I held her in my arms and called for Gabriella. She burst into the room moments later, and the look on her face was perfect. Her mouth dropped open, and she let out a piercing scream of delight. "I love it, Sissy! Grammy, Papa, look at my pink and sparkly princess room!"

"Grammy and Papa, do you mind looking after Gabriella while I help Keegan get settled?" I asked.

"Not at all, Shaky Jakey," Ranger laughed.

Mom stayed with us for the following two

weeks to help with Gabriella while Keegan was healing. By the fourth week, Keegan was able to move around the house without much difficulty, but she tired easily. By the sixth week, she was ready to get back to her normal activities. Patch cleared her to return to work on light duty only, as in, she could sit and tell others what to do, but she was to do no heavy lifting or any work with the horses.

"Promise me you'll follow Patch's instructions," I said to Keegan one more time before she got out of the car to begin her first day back at work.

"For the thousandth time, I promise. I want to avoid any setbacks just as much as you do. I'll see you this afternoon," she said and gave me a quick kiss on the cheek before she headed to the barn.

I wanted to beg her to take more time off, but I kept my mouth shut and let her go. I had been hovering over her since she was shot, and I knew she was going to blow if I didn't back off. In my defense, I loved her and watched her damn near die in front of me. I would do everything in my power to prevent that from ever happening again.

As far as I knew, she was true to her word

and followed Patch's orders. Getting back to work was exactly what she needed. After three weeks of being back at the barn, she seemed like she had recovered 100% from her injuries, and her overall mood had drastically improved. I hadn't realized how much she loved her horses and her job.

I was in my car, on the way to pick Keegan up from the barn when Duke called. I tapped a button on my steering wheel and answered. "What's up, brother?"

"You need to get your ass out to the barn," he said, and I didn't care for the urgency in his tone.

I was instantly on alert. "Why? What's wrong?" I barked, pressing harder on the gas.

"Sorry, brother. Nothing's wrong. Just something you don't want to miss. ETA?"

"About five minutes," I guessed.

"I'll try to stall. Come to the back side of the barn as soon as you get here," he said and disconnected.

Five minutes later, I jumped out of my car and rounded the corner of the barn, damn near having a heart attack from what I saw. Keegan was riding Blink, on that damn race track. I growled low in my throat.

Duke's head whipped around at the sound. "Don't say anything, brother. Just watch." When he noticed my glare, he added, "She knows what she's doing. She'll be fine out there."

I didn't comment. I crossed my arms and tried to keep my heart from beating out of my chest while I waited for whatever was to come.

Keegan and Blink had come to a stop. She wiggled around in the saddle; I presumed to get herself situated. Then, suddenly, she yelled, "Go!"

My jaw dropped open. Blink was flying down the track at a speed that seemed impossible for a horse to travel. If he tripped or she lost her grip and fell, she would be severely injured, possibly killed. Was this what she did all day?

Before I knew it, they rounded the last turn and crossed what appeared to be the finish line, though it wasn't visible to me. Hoots and hollers erupted from the sidelines, startling me. I had only seen Duke before my eyes were glued to Keegan and Blink.

Duke bumped my shoulder, "Come on; she's going to want to know the time."

I followed Duke to the track. "Why is she still riding?" I asked. My knowledge of horses was quite limited.

"She has to cool him down after working him like that," Duke explained.

"How did we do?" Keegan asked when we got closer. I saw her visibly flinch when she noticed me standing beside Duke. "Shaker, what are you doing here?"

"Picking you up from work," I said flatly.

She grimaced but didn't comment. Instead, she turned her attention to Duke. "Tell me, tell me, tell me!" Duke held up the stopwatch for her to see. "Holy shit!" she gasped. "That's—"

"Almost five seconds better than the last time," Duke finished for her, beaming from ear to ear. "Very impressive."

She finished up with Blink while various people, including Phoenix, Dash, and Ember, congratulated her on her time.

I patiently waited for her and helped her into the car when she was finished. "Where's Gabriella?" she asked.

I sighed. "She talked Ranger into taking her to the pet store. I told him no dogs, cats, snakes, spiders, or creepy reptiles, but something small would be okay."

Keegan groaned. "Oh, hell. She'll probably come home with a baby shark."

"Baby Sha—"

"If you keep singing that song, I won't fuck you for the next month."

"I'll never sing it again," I promised.

We rode in silence for the next several minutes, both of us ignoring the elephant in the car. Finally, I couldn't hold it in any longer. "You're not supposed to be riding yet."

She cleared her throat but kept her eyes pointed out the window. "Uh, about that, I was, um, cleared to ride last week."

"What? Why didn't you tell me?"

"Because I knew you didn't think I was ready, and I knew you would want to be there supervising while I was riding. I get it. I really do. But we have to get back to our normal lives."

"What exactly do you mean by that?" I asked, feeling a sense of dread start to settle in my gut.

She reached over the center console and gripped my hand. "I guess I should have said we need to start finding our normal, as a family. You know, where I go to work, you go to work, and Gabriella goes to school. And you need to stop treating me like a piece of fine china. I'm all healed up now."

"Yeah, I know. It's just, I thought I lost you that day. I don't ever want to feel like that again." I paused and shook my head. "There was so much blood. We did everything we could to help you until the paramedics got there, but then that fucking cop tasered me, and when I came back around, they had already left with you."

"You were tasered?" she shrieked.

I glanced over at her stunned face. "Yeah, for supposedly resisting arrest. You didn't know?"

"No, I didn't. Wow, that must have hurt. Did, um, never mind," she said and quickly turned away from me.

"Did what?"

"Nothing. I shouldn't ask that," she mumbled.

I pulled into the driveway and turned the car off. Then, I reached across the console and started tickling. "Ask me."

"Stooooppp! Please!" she squealed through her laughter.

"I will when you ask me your question."

"Did you," she laughed, "piss yourself?"

I let her go and looked at her incredulously. "No, I didn't piss myself. I'm a motherfucking Marine."

"How'd you get the barbs out?"

I shrugged. "Don't know. When my brain started working again, I was in handcuffs, and the barbs were gone."

"Did it hurt?"

"Fuck, yes, it hurt."

"I'm sorry that happened to you," she said softly.

"It's all good, baby," I said and pressed my lips against hers. Things were just getting heated when three sharp knocks on the window behind Keegan's head startled us both.

"Aren't you two a little old to be doing that kind of shit in the car?" Ranger asked with a disgusted look on his face.

"Sissy! Shaky Jakey! Look what Papa got me!" I cringed at the nickname Ranger had taught her as Gabriella squealed and pointed Ranger's hands. He was holding a tiny cardboard box with a few small holes in the top.

Keegan laughed. "Gabriella, we can't see what's in the box, so why don't you tell us."

Gabriella beamed at her sister. "Mice!"

"Mice?" we both asked at the same time.

Ranger cleared his throat. "She thought one would be lonely and asked if she could have two. So, we got two males. I've got their cage and everything else they need in the truck," he explained and handed the box to Keegan.

Keegan eyed it warily and carefully took the box. Moments later, she was giggling and cooing. She pointed to one of the holes, "Look at its cute little nose!"

I made a mental note to keep Keegan away from pet stores. Apparently, she was a sucker for animals.

We spent the next few hours putting together the cage and getting the little rodents set up in their new home, which Keegan referred to as a Mouse McMansion.

"They are kind of cute," Keegan mused.

"Yeah, as long as they stay in their cage," I grumbled.

"Hey, at least they didn't come home with a pig. Just the other day, Gabriella told me she wanted a pet pig."

"Just saying, something like that will live at your barn, not at our house."

"Agreed."

"I can have a pet pig?" Gabriella squealed in delight behind us.

"Fucking hell," I muttered.

CHAPTER TWENTY-SEVEN

Keegan

Later that night, Shaker asked if I would be okay with Gabriella spending Saturday night with his mother.

"You mean her fairy grandmother?" I asked, causing him to chuckle. "It's fine with me. Does she have something fun planned?"

"I'm sure she will, but that's not why I asked. Kellan is getting patched in Saturday, and there'll be a party at the clubhouse afterward."

"Oh, that sounds fun," I said and immediately started planning.

Even though I'd flat out told Shaker to stop treating me like a delicate piece of China, he was still doing it. Sure, we'd had sex since the shooting, but it was what I would call gentle lovemaking, and I wanted him to fuck me.

The next day, I called Jacquelyn and asked if Gabriella could spend Friday night with her, too. She readily agreed and offered to pick her up right after school. However, she did refuse to take the mice along for the weekend, despite Gabriella's incessant begging.

As soon as they were out the door, I started getting things ready. I knew Shaker would be home later than usual because he had Church at the clubhouse, and I planned on using that extra time to the fullest. I started by hopping in the shower and giving everything a good shave.

Tossing my hair into a messy bun, I pulled on a pair of shorty shorts and an old tank top to wear while I got dinner started. Once everything was in the crockpot, I went back to our bedroom to finish getting ready.

After applying my makeup, I got to work on my hair. I had just finished drying it when I heard the front door open. Crap! He was home early. I looked down at my body and made a quick decision. Jerking my shorts off, I tossed them across the room, leaving me in my threadbare white tank top and a black thong. I grabbed the handcuffs I'd purchased earlier in the week and quickly secured my hands behind my back. Just as I heard his boots outside the bedroom door, I dropped to my knees beside the bed and spread my legs wide.

"Keegan?" he called as he pushed the bedroom door open.

I didn't say anything, just waited for him to notice me. And it didn't take long. He rounded the bed, and a devious grin appeared on his face when he saw me. "What are you doing?"

"Waiting for you."

He glanced over his shoulder. "Where's Gabriella?"

"She's spending the whole weekend with your mother."

His grin grew even wider. "I see." He dropped to his knees in front of me and cupped my pussy with his big hand. "Were you planning something?"

"Yes," I answered on a moan because he unexpectedly filled me with two fingers.

"Tell me what you have planned, baby," he ordered as he began sliding his fingers in and out of my channel.

"I, uh, I, oh, fuck that feels good. I, uh, want you to fuck me. Hard. Rough. Dirty. Please," I miraculously managed to say.

"Keegan—," he started, but I cut him off.

"Don't you dare tell me no. I'm fine. The doctor said I could resume all normal activity. Now, stop being a pussy and fuck mine."

Without a word, he yanked my tank top up over my bare breasts and tried to pull it over my head. When my arms didn't move, he peered over my shoulder at my cuffed hands.

Abruptly, he stood and turned away from me. "Where are the keys?"

"Shaker?" I asked, unsure of what upset him.

"Keys, Keegan!" he barked.

"On the nightstand. Behind me," I said shakily.

"Can you get them off?" he asked.

"Yes," I said and pressed the quick release lever to remove them. I also pulled my shirt back into place and righted my panties. "Okay, they're off."

Before he turned back to face me, he started to explain, "I can't do handcuffs. If you want to play with restraints, we'll have to use something else."

It took me a minute, but I recalled the story Harper told me while we were shopping. "Because of Hilarie?"

He whirled around with a scowl on his face. "Fuck, no. Why would you even ask that?"

"Uh, because she kidnapped you and tried to rape you."

He shook his head. "It doesn't have anything to do with her." He crossed the room and sat beside me on the bed. Placing his hand on my bare thigh, he said, "As soon as I saw the cuffs, it took me back to when you were shot. My hands were cuffed behind my back, and all I could do was stare at the pool of your blood on the floor. I have never been that scared in my entire life, and I don't ever want to feel that way again."

I sniffed. "Understood. Are you hungry? Dinner should be ready."

He placed a finger under my chin and tipped my head back so he could drop a kiss to my lips. "Yeah, I'm hungry. Let's eat, and then we'll try this again."

"Can I ask you something first?"

He chuckled. "You just did." At my glare, he added, "You know you can ask me anything."

"Why haven't you tried to do what you used to do with me?" I asked, keeping my eyes focused on my lap.

"Not sure what you're asking, babe."

I cleared my throat, but couldn't bring myself

to look at him. "You know what I'm asking."

"Oh, are you asking why I haven't fucked your ass?"

"Yeah, that," I mumbled.

"Because I don't want to."

"Well, at least you're honest," I snapped and rose to my feet.

"Aw, shit, Keegan. I didn't mean it like that," he said and yanked me into his lap. "Before, when I made that promise to myself, it was a means to an end. Honestly, it's not my preference."

"Bullshit! You developed a problem because of it." I tried to get up, but he tightened his hold on me.

"Despite what Harper thinks, I actually do listen to some of the things she says. And, for lack of a better description, let's just say I mentally blocked all things pussy. Well, at least until your spell-casting snatch showed up," he said and pressed his lips against my shoulder.

"So, you're telling me you don't want to have anal sex with me because my hoo-ha hexed you?"

He kissed his way up to my jaw and breathed me in. "I'm saying I love your pussy. If you want me to fuck your ass, I will. We can try anything you want to, but I'm telling you right now, nothing will ever top your cunt."

"We can try anything?" I asked innocently. He nodded with a smile. "Even a devil's three-way?"

"When I said *we*, I meant the two of us and only the two of us. There will never be anyone else in our bedroom. Ever," he declared.

I couldn't hold back my laughter. "You should've seen your face!"

"I ought to spank your ass for that," he grumbled.

"Oh, maybe we should start a list of things to try," I suggested.

He stood with me in his arms and headed for the kitchen. "Food, Keegan. We need to eat. I have a feeling it's going to be a long night."

"Wait!" I protested. "Let me grab my shorts."

"Nope, you're eating like that. Actually, let's lose the tank top, too."

So, I sat at our dinner table in nothing but a black thong and tried to focus on eating instead of the steadily growing ache between my legs.

Shaker told me to remain seated while he cleared the table. He took his sweet time, and when he finally returned, I was flushed and breathing heavily.

He smirked but didn't come to me. Instead,

he sat in his chair and said two words. "Come 'ere."

I sprang from my chair, ready to jump into his lap, when he nodded his head toward the table. "Crawl."

Any other time, I would have questioned him, but I was so worked up, I was ready to do whatever he asked of me. Without hesitation, I climbed on top of the table and crawled across to him on all fours.

He took my lips in a quick kiss when I reached him. "Good, now let me see how wet your pretty pussy is."

I moved to a sitting position and shamelessly spread my legs for his viewing pleasure. His grin turned feral. "Keep your eyes on mine and your hands on the table." He didn't wait for my agreement before slowly sliding two fingers into my slick channel.

I sucked in a breath and arched my back, but kept my eyes locked with his as he continued to slide his fingers in and out at a tortuously slow pace. He wasn't touching my clit, and it was driving me mad.

Sensing I was nearing my breaking point, he stood and captured one nipple with his mouth, sucking hard. He gave my other nipple the same treatment and released it with a pop.

With his teeth nipping at my neck, he rumbled, "You asked for it." Suddenly, his fingers were gone, and I was filled with him. Without pause, he began thrusting with a force I wasn't expecting. I reached for his shoulders to steady myself, but he stopped me. "Hands on the table." Gripping the edge, I held on while he gave me what I wanted.

"Love watching those tits bounce while your cunt's clamping down on my cock. Fucking give it to me, Keegan."

And I did. I exploded into pulsating waves of pleasure as electric tingles of passion coursed through me.

"Fuck, yeah, baby," Shaker groaned as his rhythm faltered, and he reached his own climax.

To my surprise, he pulled out, bent me over the table, and pushed back inside. "Not anywhere near fucking done with you," he stated.

And he wasn't.

EPILOGUE

Shaker

D ragging my ass out of bed was the last thing I wanted to do, but I couldn't miss Church. So, I got myself showered and dressed, told my wife I would see her at the party later, and went to the clubhouse.

As expected, Kellan was voted in unanimously. Badger took his prospect cut, but Phoenix didn't hand him his club cut. Instead, he held up a hand to stop any comments, and Kellan's face paled. "Ranger," Phoenix said with a nod to the back of the room.

Ranger walked to the front and stood beside Phoenix. His face was a mask of seriousness. "Brothers, Prospect Kellan went above and beyond for the club. His attention to detail and quick thinking saved my grandbaby and Shaker's wife several times. He took a bullet for her, and he stopped her life from pouring out of her with his bare hands. Welcome to the club, Savior."

Phoenix held out his cut, and Kellan promptly slipped it over his shoulders as the room erupted into cheers.

"All right, let's get this party started!" Phoenix bellowed.

As expected, the Old Ladies were in the common room, all sitting in what they had recently deemed their section of the clubhouse, which was nothing more than a particular corner of the common room.

After getting a drink from the bar, I found a seat and waited for Keegan to come join me, which she did fifteen minutes later when the group dispersed. She sat herself in my lap and rested her head on my shoulder.

"You okay, wifey?"

"Yeah," she said wistfully. "It's just so nice to see everyone happy."

When I looked around the room, at first glance, I saw the single guys getting ready to have a night of fun – a few taking shots at the bar, others getting ready to have their asses handed to them by Ranger at the pool tables, and one or two already engaged with a club whore. But beyond that, I saw Phoenix with one arm around Annabelle's shoulders while his other hand rested on their twins in her ever-growing belly. They were talking with Badger who was standing with his arms wrapped around Macy from behind. Duke and Reese were by the bar with their noses and foreheads pressed together, grinning like fools at each other. Dash and Ember were on one of the couches, her swollen ankles propped on his leg while he rubbed her feet and she caressed her baby bump. Harper had her arms and legs wrapped around Carbon as he carried her out of the common room. And I had my wife perched in my lap and plastered to my chest. Kissing her temple, I squeezed her tightly, "Yeah, baby, it fucking is."

Also by Teagan Brooks

Blackwings MC
Dash
Duke
Phoenix
Carbon